Sitting with Gold
The Stories

Corrine Coleman

DEDICATION

To my dear husband, Kenny, for granting me the serenity to write; for the memories; for our home which is always wherever we are together. You are the hardest working man I know. You are the silent giver – the one who stands in the background allowing us all to shine. Before you there were tears. Now, there are flowers, too.

CONTENTS

ACKNOWLEDGMENTS

My stories have a way of filling me up and draining me out all at the same time. I wouldn't have it any other way. The beautiful, intricate people that surround me have always been an inspiration. Just by giving a part of themselves they have touched me and my characters allowing us to flourish.

Christine & Craig: Things that have the ability to tear people apart have always brought us closer. The two of you are at the core of everything. You are the family I started with before all the others got added on. There is something so sacred about the knowledge that, with every step I take, there are two people in the world who have been there with me from the beginning.

Sanda: You have been my greatest fan. You never let me doubt myself and you always know just what to say when the words cannot be found. I admire your perseverance and your profound courage. You are the bright star in my sky. You are the one always forcing me to look deeper into myself.

Mira & Christopher: I didn't realize I could love so deeply until each of you fell asleep in my arms. Mira, you are riveting and unique. You, with your splendid, analytic mind have a love for all creatures and a passion for creativity. You will do great things and you will do them with heart. Christopher, you are rarely seen without a smile on your face. I watch you with others and you are magnetic – you have that special something which will follow you for a lifetime.

Leigh & Evelyn: Before you there was an empty place inside me. When I fell in love with your father I opened up my heart to the two most beautiful human beings I can imagine. Leigh, with your unbeatable ambition and talent - you're a superstar in your own right. Evie, with your quiet magnificence – you're a deep thinker, like me; a force to be reckoned with. The lessons you both have taught me are invaluable.

Nicky: You are the epitome of a good person. You gave me something I will never forget: a place in our family and an important role in your life. Caring for you has been the easiest thing to do. I'm proud to call you my stepson.

1 DEAR ROGER

Dear Roger,

By the time you read this I will be gone. It might interest you to know that on the day I wrote this letter you were outside, fussing with the weeds in the yard.

I was in the spare bedroom, sitting on the yellow chaise-lounge, watching you from behind the green, velvet curtains I had chosen for the room.

Why velvet? you had asked on the day I was hanging them - though, you never much bothered with decor.

Because it reminds me of drapes I saw in a movie once, I said.

Who notices curtains in a movie?

At the time I wanted to point out that I do. I wanted to remind you that I had always been one to focus on the details - whereas you easily missed them.

In the movie, Gone with the Wind, I said, *the velvet drapes were turned into a dress for Scarlett - because she lost everything and did not have the money for a proper gown. She wanted to convince Captain Butler to help her.*

Even as I spoke the words I knew that they were foreign to you. You didn't watch such films. You didn't care about expanding your tastes or opening your mind. You didn't come with me to the opera. You didn't read literature - or appreciate art. You were fine simply existing. You were happy when the grass was green. You were happy with your nightly television sitcom - and a cold beer in hand. You didn't have an empty space in your heart - one that grew larger through the years and thirsted, without being quenched. It was me who suffered like that.

So, I was behind the curtains, my fingers grasping a small piece of the thick material - just enough to pull them aside so that I could see you without being discovered.

Earlier, when I glanced outside, there was a cloud of dirt surrounding you. Your face and t-shirt were damp with sweat and your pale skin was pink with determination. The lawn was too dry - it hadn't really been cared for in a while because you had badly sprained your ankle a few months back - and so, it was a struggle for you to mow it.

Now, with a pen against my lips, I observed as you tugged at the dandelions. Even though I couldn't hear you, I imagined you were cursing them. You would be out there for hours - because you were accustomed to working hard. When you stood to stretch, I noticed your posture was getting worse. And that your belly was round and protruding.

Still, you were not a man that didn't get noticed.

When we did go out to eat, which was rare, you would clean up well. Once your shirt was tucked in and your shiny shoes were on you would raise your head higher and your pale-green eyes would take the forefront; your chiseled jaw-line more apparent. Women *did* notice you. Maybe not as much as they used to, but they noticed. So, it's not that you weren't an attractive man. Outwardly - if one didn't know of your social awkwardness or of your inability to keep any negative thoughts to yourself - you were, especially in your younger years, quite appealing.

It's just difficult for me to remember a moment when I longed for you - *really* longed for you, the way I longed for him. Maybe it was because your smile was lacking - it never really reached your eyes. And almost immediately, I recognized that. It had always bothered me - your indifference. Still, you were safe. Isn't that what they all say? Maybe. But, you have always been a good, honest man. And, I was a girl from a broken family. As you know, I never knew my father. So - like the old story goes, I longed for a solid man. I suppose I had been at odds with myself. I desperately needed a man that would never leave. And I got him. And it stifled me.

It's not that I never loved you. That would be a foolish thing to say. It would negate all that we had. I have fond memories of you - like when you taught me how to fish during the years you were still courting me, or the way your face shone when you first held our daughter. There were many cold evenings that you kept me warm. And there were many empty moments that you filled. You have been more than only a chapter of my life. You *are* my life. You are my entire life because before you there was only a blank page. Even now, you are still ever-present in my thoughts. Even when I try to push you to the back of my mind, you emerge - as if you know what I'm doing and will not allow it.

His name was Sean. Sean would never be a man that one would consider conventionally attractive. He was only slightly taller than me - he didn't tower over me the way you did. He had a nose that was a bit too prominent and his hair was beginning to thin. He was in decent shape but he wasn't without flaws. He was an average looking man and I met him on an average day. But, this doesn't mean he was an average man.

It was a Sunday morning and it had been raining. You were sitting in your favorite brown chair reading the newspaper. You were still in the colorful, patterned boxer shorts you slept in and your graying, curly hair was wildly unkempt. You were sipping your coffee and I remember thinking how odd it was that the scent seemed to emanate off of you earlier, during sex, and you hadn't yet had your morning cup.

We rarely had sex in the mornings - because I liked

to sleep in. And I suppose it didn't help that I have always been a bit irritable early in the day. That morning, though, you were unrelenting - pushing your body, hard, against mine and probing me, as if I was your specimen. I gave in just so you would leave me alone.

I had been having sex with your for twenty-five years. And it was always the same. You would begin touching me, randomly. Then, I would lay back, in a spot on your side of the bed, and you would enter me. You would kiss my cheek and my forehead - because each time you went for my lips, I would turn my head away. And each time you tried to look into my eyes, I avoided your stare.

I suppose the dissatisfaction in our sex life was my fault just as much as it was yours. It had become a chore. And chores were never fun. But, I'm getting off the topic - as you say I always do.

So, I left you that day to go to the market. I was wearing grey sweatpants - the ones I would normally never be seen in - and a pale blue cotton blouse. I threw the yellow, over-sized rain-jacket over my body and ran out the door believing I would be back in ten minutes. We were out of bottled water - and I refused to drink tap - so, the mission, for the moment, was to get myself something to drink. When I look back I can't help but find that ironic.

The minute I walked out the front door, I stepped into a puddle and my sneakers and socks were instantly drenched. The rain was coming down so hard that I wondered if it was actually hail - and I pulled my hood over my head, tying it tightly to my scalp.

When I entered our practical five-year old station wagon, I was happy to be safe from the storm, but the smell of nicotine that was ever-present - because you couldn't stop smoking in the car - made me cringe. It always made me cringe. And, the funny thing was that it was a part of you. It was a part of your scent.

I began the drive down the long, winding road,

into town. I remember thinking that the road seemed so desolate - as though there were not houses behind the trees that lined it. Perhaps, in a way, the road mirrored my feelings on that day: I was unknown.

When I was finally inside the store, I was dripping, and my sneakers made muddy trails behind me. For a few aisles I didn't run into another person at all. I lingered, lazily, in front of the magazines and books thinking about how nice it would be to curl up in front of the fireplace and read a novel with a glass of red wine beside me. But I knew the minute you were done reading your newspaper, you would turn the television on - at an unbearable volume because, though you denied it, your hearing had gotten worse in the last few years - and it would remain that way for the entire day. This was your Sunday routine. And, so, even if I went upstairs - or into the bedroom - it would never really be quiet.

I suppose I had been flipping through the pages of a book when I sensed that I wasn't alone. There wasn't a sound - which was odd - or, maybe there was, but I was too engrossed in my thoughts to have heard it. It was more like a feeling. When I glanced behind me there was a man standing there - a dark, studious-looking man. That's really the only way I can describe my immediate impression of him. He was dark - his hair, his eyes, his skin. And his face had an expression of acute interest on it - as though it didn't matter what else he had going on, he was fully focused on the moment and what he was doing presently.

He wasn't looking at me. He was examining the books in front of us. He remained behind me, I assume to give me space. Perhaps I had been leaning against the rack, preventing anyone from passing through. Perhaps I had silently declared the small area as my own and he was too polite to say anything.

He had a thin, grey jacket on and his arms were folded across his chest. He stood straight and evenly with his legs slightly apart and his black hair was damp and matted against his olive skin.

I moved to get out of his way. When I did this, he spoke.

"It's fine," he said, in a low, soft tone. But it wasn't unkind. It was a friendly voice. "I can see."

I smiled, quickly, noticing how vivid his dark eyes appeared. They were nearly black - yet, they appeared brighter than yours.

It is said that these things occur mainly because the right circumstances present themselves. I was a woman, nearing forty-five, in a marriage that had long lost its luster. I was hungry for change - for a feeling in my belly that I hadn't felt since I was a girl. I was cold and I was wet, envisioning a roaring fire and a nice bottle of wine. Wasn't that a recipe for romance?

He was a stranger who happened to be out on the same dreary Sunday. He was interested in books - it didn't matter what kind. His eyes held wisdom within them - and there was something so mysteriously familiar about him. Does that make sense? Probably not. It's always difficult to explain what goes on in a woman's heart - thoughts become jumbled. Sometimes, when one tries to translate feelings into words they just fall short.

Anyway, he wasn't overly impressive in any of the physical attributes but he was quite comfortable in his own skin. It was easy to see that he had confidence. And, he didn't need to smile with his mouth. He smiled with his eyes. Yes, Roger. He smiled with his eyes.

"Are you looking for a particular book?" I asked, surprising myself. It really wasn't any of my business.

"Not really," he said, "Just browsing." Then, he gestured toward the book in my hand. "Quite a steamy read you have there." And he chuckled.

I glanced at the novel I held. The cover art was of a strikingly beautiful couple - seemingly naked - entwined in a deep, sensual embrace.

I felt the heat on my cheeks. I quickly placed the book back on the shelf. "They're - they don't really have much of a selection," I said. Then, I reached for a strand of my red hair and twisted it, nervously. It was a habit you despised.

He smiled. "I'm just kidding," he said. "I didn't mean to embarrass you."

I looked away, briefly - but my smile didn't leave. I really liked that he said that. Not only because it was kind - but, because it was nice to have an emotion of mine acknowledged. You had stopped noticing me a long time ago. Truth is, you didn't notice a lot of things. It's not that you were a cold person - you simply lacked the ability to read people well.

So, when I think about it - because, I have thought of it, many times - it was only within moments that a connection was made. That's all the time it took for everything to change.

I could have arrived at the store an hour later - or, maybe even a few minutes earlier. Then, our little interaction would not have occurred. If it had been a sunny day, maybe I wouldn't have dreamt up the perfect romantic recipe and, instead, went for a jog. If I wasn't damp from the rain and feeling plain and unattractive - maybe I wouldn't have been so easily enthralled. Or maybe I'm simply fooling myself and it all would have happened anyway.

"Do you live around here?" he asked. And I found myself searching his hands for a wedding band. I was disappointed to find one.

"Yes, just north of here. Up the hill." And then, because I wanted him to stay, "What about you?"

He seemed to be studying my face; reading me. I understood this because I often did it. I often searched people's faces for answers. I trusted faces more than words. "I actually live in New York," he said, "I'm here just for a few weeks. I'm house-hunting."

"Oh. Well - it's just lovely here. Really."

He nodded. "I know. I lived here as a boy. I have great memories. Me and my dog, Bosco - we spent a lot of time at the lake."

I giggled - like a school girl. Then, I sighed. From the first day we moved here, fifteen years ago, I was enamored with the little Pennsylvania town. Did you know how much I loved it? Did you know how excited I was to start my life? *It's so far from everything*, you had said. You didn't like the seclusion. But, it was all we could afford. And, so you settled. And I suppose, my love for the place became clouded with your disdain for it.

"It's a beautiful lake," I said. "Have you and your wife found anything yet?" And it was silly for me to mention her. He wore a wedding band. He was married. What was I really asking?

He didn't answer me right away. There was something about the silences with him - they were never empty. With you, silences were always silent.

"I'm Sean," he said. And he reached his hand out to me.

"Christine," I said, taking his hand. His fingers wrapped around mine. There was an instant jolt.

"Are you married?" he asked, in a near-whisper. There was something so urgent in his voice - as if he needed to know; as if he had suddenly become consumed with an intense hunger.

I glanced at my finger and his eyes followed mine. I stared at the small diamond ring you had proposed to me with so many years ago in my mother's kitchen. You had worked hard for that ring, I knew. So, it didn't bother me that you never thought to buy a wedding band to complement it. I never took the ring off. Looking at it in that moment, though, I saw how yellow and dirty it had become.

For a few moments I didn't look back up at him. I thought, perhaps, I was imagining something between us that was not really there. I inspected my muddy sneakers and the stain on my pants. What could he possibly want with me?

"My wife is not with me," he said, quickly. "I'm staying just down the road."

When my eyes met his I saw everything. He wasn't being presumptuous. No - he had already seen, in my face, what I wanted - what I needed. And he wasn't being perverse. I didn't, not even for a moment, suspect that he did this sort of thing often. No, what was occurring in that second had been unexpected for the both of us. Delightfully unexpected.

"Let's go," I said, feeling the heat prickling beneath my skin. And he didn't hesitate. Instead, he placed his hand on the small of my back and gently guided me out the door. I remember thinking about the water I had left stranded in the cart. I didn't need it anymore.

It isn't necessary for me to go into all the details about what occurred when we reached his motel room. But I want you to understand it, so details are important.

We went for a purpose and that purpose was filled. It was savored. For hours, I stayed with him, undressed beneath the sheets. He kissed my freckles and he asked about my scars. He ran his fingers against the ripples on my belly - the ripples I was gifted with after having our daughter. He told me I was beautiful, even beneath the unforgiving fluorescent light. He held my hands, tightly, as he slid his damp body on top of mine. When I sneezed during our lovemaking we laughed, loudly, like teenagers who didn't have a care in the world. Afterwards, we remained naked and intertwined - like the couple on the book cover. And we read magazines together as if we had been doing it for years.

When the sun began to set I didn't want to leave him.

"I think I fell in love today," I said. And it didn't

feel odd, at all, to say. It felt like the most natural thing in the world.

"I know," he said, "Am I supposed to resume my life as if this never happened?"

"It's impossible," I told him, "I need to see you again."

He nodded. "Tomorrow?"

I didn't doubt it. "Yes. Early, please."

He kissed me and his sweet breath lingered on my lips the whole ride home.

When I pulled up to the house I imagined you frantic with worry. I had a list of excuses in my mind that I would give you. I would pick one, depending on how angry you were.

But when I walked through the door you were still in the same spot I had left you in. You were snoring. I couldn't believe it. I left you in the morning to buy some bottled water. The entire day had passed before I returned without anything at all. And you had never even noticed I was gone.

I turned off the television and covered you with a blanket. Then, I changed into my nightdress without showering. I didn't want to wash his scent off of me.

You awoke around midnight. I heard you fumbling through the kitchen for food. When you finally crawled into bed beside me, you were restless and I felt you moving closer to me. I pretended to be asleep. You kissed my neck - not because you were feeling affectionate - but, because you wanted sex. You never just kissed me to kiss me. It was always meant to mean that you wanted sex.

I wondered if you could sense that something was different. Perhaps his warm, musky fragrance still remained - and perhaps you had noticed it. Would you have thought, for a moment, that your devoted wife could spend an entire day making love to a stranger? Would you have imagined that somebody else could desire me so much?

Eventually, with no response from me, you turned away. And before long you were snoring again.

I wanted to feel guilty. I wanted to be angry with myself - because weren't those the appropriate emotions?

But I didn't feel guilty. Not then. I was elated. I felt liberated. For years my thoughts had bored me. Life had become mundane. Sometimes, there were days that seemed to drag on so long, I would wish them away - only to realize that there was another one to follow.

Sean had given me so much in such a short time. He had filled my mind with glorious complexities. I was churning in my infancy. I fell asleep, that night, just on the edge of ecstasy.

In the morning you were running late. *I'm so tired*, you had said. And it was such a contrast from what I was feeling. I had such energy that morning - I felt vividly alive. But, I remained under the covers because I didn't want you to notice any of it.

When you left, I dialed the motel room and Sean answered the phone right away. I brought him breakfast and we ate it in bed. Then, we undressed quickly and took a long, morning shower together. I think it was one of the most erotic things I have ever experienced. I remember his wet fingers wrapped around the soapy bar as it glided in slow, circular motions around my belly, and then my breasts - and his body was warm and slippery behind me. His lips trailed down my skin, pausing for slow, titillating seconds, as I swayed in frantic, ravenous motion. The steam enveloped us like a thick, protective shield, and we welcomed it as we lost ourselves in the sensuous exploration of each other.

I had created a world of my own. For the next two weeks I went to sleep with you in the evenings and I gave my days to him.

We never left his motel room - for the town was small and we couldn't take the chance. But, we experienced more in that room than I have in a lifetime, with you.

We danced, slow and close, to sultry jazz tunes heard through an old cassette player. We lit candles when the days were dark and stormy - and made love near the opened windows so that the rain could come through in trickles upon our skin. We dined on blankets on the old carpeted floor - and drank champagne in plastic cups. We read passages from our favorite books, and we watched old movies, naked, in bed. I sang to him - did you know that I used to sing when I was a girl? - and he played the guitar that he had pulled out from a blanket in the back of his truck. *It has always been a hobby*, he had said, *it's nice to play for someone again.*

He never finished his house hunting. And I fell behind on my chores. And we never talked about leaving our homes and being with each other. We both had lives that couldn't be interrupted. We both cared for our spouses and didn't want to hurt them. We both had children. His were still young.

When the day came for him to leave it felt as though somebody was twisting a blade into my belly and dragging it, slowly, to my heart.

"There are so many things I want you to know," I said, through a voice that couldn't stop cracking. I wanted him to understand. And, I didn't know how to say goodbye.

He held me close for a long, long time. "Let's not talk about love," he said, "Because isn't it just a word to us now?" And he was right. Love had lost its meaning. "It's more," he said, "It doesn't need to be defined."

And it made perfect sense. To me. It isn't something that anybody else may ever understand. Even in this letter, though I try hard to convey what occurred between us, I simply cannot do it justice.

We parted with the knowledge that we wouldn't see each other again. He would no longer be moving his family nearby. *How can I, now?* he had asked, *she would never stand a chance.*

I stood on the graveled road, in front of the motel, and I watched him drive away. I stayed there, frozen, for many minutes. Perhaps I hoped he would return. I don't know what I would have done if he had.

Later that evening, when you arrived home, I felt the slow draining of my energy - the energy that had encompassed me for the last two weeks. And, I didn't want to think about the long life waiting ahead of me.

I made you dinner - chicken and peas. And we ate together. For the first time I poured us both a glass of wine. You seemed a little surprised - as we never had wine with dinner - but you were pleased. I surveyed your face as you ate. The lines around your mouth were getting deep. And the creases around your eyes were really aging you. Your chapped lips were dark from the wine and you ate your food as though you hadn't eaten in weeks. For the first time, since meeting Sean, I felt a pang in my heart - for you. Perhaps I needed to redirect my pain.

You were just a regular, decent man - a flawed man, inside. But, weren't we all flawed inside? You didn't abuse me in any way. You came home every night and woke up with me every morning. You took care of our home and you worked hard every day. You had been a good father to our daughter - and she had become successful, because you had always made sure she wasn't lazy - you kept her motivated. Perhaps you believed she could do the things you always wanted to do, but never did. She had surpassed us in many ways. But, I know it wasn't because of me. I had been a bit indolent. I had been a bit depressed through the years.

I had always, inwardly, blamed you for everything that was wrong in my life. But in that moment I realized it had never been your fault.

I had wanted to be something bigger - a singer, an actress, a writer. It didn't matter which. I wanted to be something grandiose. *That's a fool's dream*, you had said.

You didn't support my vision - but, how could you? You came from a long line of realists. You were taught to work for your money not to dream away your life. You didn't understand that mindset. But, you never prevented me from doing anything. I prevented myself. Perhaps my insecurities and fears pushed me to blame you because it was easier to accept if I removed the blame from myself. It was easier to believe that you wanted me to remain a housewife.

It's so strange when clarity occurs.

Did you have dreams that I didn't know of? Weren't you a happier man - a boy, really - when we first met? Hadn't you been passionate about nature - and the outdoors? Did I ever really make an effort to join you on your camping trips? Would I have enjoyed you more, if I did? Did you ever love another woman?

No. It was only me you loved. In your own way. You weren't a charming man. You weren't overly attentive and you didn't spoil me. But, you desired me. You took care of me because I never took the steps to take care of myself. You let me believe I had been a good mother - but you more than made up for what I lacked as a parent.

I suppose after that night things could have been different for us. And they were - a little different.

We continued to have wine with our evening meal - because we both enjoyed the idea. Why hadn't we done it before? When we made love I kissed you on the lips and I made an effort to look into your eyes - to see you. I noticed that you didn't sit in your brown chair for hours at a time on Sundays anymore. Instead, you would find moments to join me on the couch. And once in a while, you would plant a kiss on my cheek - just because.

These were not major changes. Our life was still pretty much the same. They were small things. But they were significant things. And it didn't escape my awareness that, between all of our tiny, kind gestures, Sean was still firmly planted at the base of my mind. It's possible that he was the reason for all of it - as was my desire to hold on to that feeling. I was afraid to let go of the happiness - and of falling into a cold, black hole, for good.

It was almost as if I was working to survive. But, in that survival mode I recognized so much of what had happened between you and I.

About a month and a half later I found out I was pregnant.

That's right. Pregnant.

I didn't, for one moment, think that my missed period was a pregnancy. I thought - menopause. It had to be! My own mother had already finished menopause by the time she was my age. So - it wasn't odd to be irregular. It was normal.

I began reading numerous articles on the subject - to prepare myself. It was necessary, in my mind, to understand what my body was going to be up against. I'm not going to lie and tell you that the thought wasn't disheartening. It was just another reminder that my youth was long behind me. And, after feeling so fresh during those weeks with Sean, the idea only further exasperated the impact of his absence.

When I came across an article about a woman who had carried babies well into her late forties, I took a home pregnancy test. The result slapped me into reality. A myriad of emotions followed.

I had no idea who the father was. In my heart, I'm sorry to say, I wanted it to be Sean. Because, then I would have a part of him with me forever.

But, the baby could have just as easily been yours. And - did I really want to be a mother again? Did I really want to go down that road for a second time - when I wasn't so good at it the first time?

For days I retreated to the bedroom early and cried myself to sleep.

Then, on one morning - perhaps because the sun

had slipped through the closed drapes and onto my face, warming me - I convinced myself that it was fate. It was Sean's child and this was a product of our love. It was meant to be; something that simply had to happen.

With that mindset, I felt lighter - happy, even. And I would find myself humming through the housework. And I would stand in front of the mirror, naked, running my fingers across my belly - thinking of Sean's fingers sliding against my skin. I would have a boy - I was sure of it. And I would name him Sean. And you would be a good father to him. He would be well taken care of. And nobody would ever have to know my secret.

I was going to tell you after my first ultrasound. I was going to make it special this time - for the first time I shared this kind of news with you, I had only been a girl. I was going to make you a wonderful dinner - roasted chicken, broccoli florets and garlic mashed potatoes with warm rolls. And when I told you, your face would brighten the way it did when you found out you were having a daughter. And we would both have something to look forward to again. And this time I would do it right.

But the ultrasound could detect no heartbeat. The pregnancy had terminated.

This brings me to today. It has been one year since I lost the baby. And with that loss came the realization that no matter how hard I try, our life together will always be only skimming the surface of contentment. My life, Roger, has never been whole. And I don't believe yours has, either.

We are not truly happy. You may believe you are, because living this way is all you have ever known. But, Roger, there is a whole world out there. We have many years left to live. Is this how you want to spend them?

Perhaps when you read this you will be frantically nodding - screaming out the word *Yes!* - and your disbelief, maybe even grief - will be overwhelming. And I am so sorry to have caused you this anguish.

I didn't write this letter to hurt you. I wrote this letter to help you understand why I must go.

It isn't because I have loved another man. That experience was a necessity - a blast of cold water that had long been overdue; one that I will forever be grateful for. I am quite aware of the possibility that those cherished moments with Sean were fleeting - and that they may not have lasted past the old motel room, anymore than we would have lasted past this stagnant house, where our crutches lie. So I am not leaving you because of Sean.

And, Roger, it has little to do with you or with my love for you, which, as I have pointed out, has also existed. I hope when you read this you will be confident in that fact, and you will realize that I have loved you in the same way that you have loved me - with the limits we have placed on ourselves. And this is nobody's fault. It is simply the way the wind blew. Like I spoke about earlier - circumstances are all too powerful. Moments passed, cannot be taken back. They all played a part in the path that led us here. And we became the people we are because we didn't fight to take another path.

I am leaving us because I need to find me. Perhaps this sounds like a cliché. And I am sure you are shaking your head - yelling out about what a fool I am to give up all the years we have shared together. I am sure you are thinking that my actions are that of immaturity - and that I will be back when I realize I am a middle-aged woman with nowhere to go. Perhaps you think I'm having a mid-life crisis.

I know my words have not yet fully hit you. And that you will read this letter again and again before you even begin to comprehend what I am saying.

This is why I have covered so many details. I envision you, one day, jumping up from your brown chair and fiercely pulling the plug on your old television set -

because something inside finally triggered you to understand me. And something inside finally triggered you to want more.

My mind is very clear right now. I want you to know this. And I am very calm. I am putting this letter in an envelope at the bottom of your office drawer. I know you clean this drawer out every six months. This gives me a little more time to find a job - and a place - so that I can have a fair start when I go. I do not expect anything from you.

Certainly, when the moment is right, I will let our daughter know of my decision. And she will tell you before you find this letter. And you will think it unfair - and perhaps you will hate me and think me a coward for not facing you and telling you directly.

But we both know I could not have done it that way. You would have convinced me to stay. And I would have - out of pity.

This is something that I must do. For the both of us.

You will not be seeing me for a long time, Roger. It may even be years. But - rest assured that you will see me again. For, we share much more than a daughter. We have ties that will keep us bound for a lifetime.

When I do meet you again, I want to see you laughing. I want to see the sparkle lighting up your tired eyes. I want to see you standing straighter - allowing me to experience all of your marvelous height. I don't want to see only half of a man anymore.

I want you to have met another woman - one that will give you the burst of energy you need to truly know another person. I want to see you as a man, in love.

I hope when you see me, you see the woman I always wanted to be. I hope I will be invigorated with the kind of freedom that one can only find on the inside. And,

I hope we can hug each other, tightly, and find peace in the knowledge that one of us changed direction so that we both could be led to a better, more beautiful world.

I am sorry for my deception - and for the pain you are feeling right at this moment. I know you will heal sooner than you think.

Goodbye, my dear friend.

With love,
Christine

2 LOSING A BUCK

I loved him. That was all there was to it. He was a visionary. He was an artist. When he spoke, I was transported. When he kissed me it was always because he absolutely had to. We didn't finish each other's sentences. We challenged each other. Our conversations were rocky journeys up tall, interesting hills. The scenery was always captivating. But, the ride was never easy.

We met very simply. It was at a local cafe, not far from New York City. I was writing, long-hand, in my thick, green notebook. He was typing, ferociously, on his small, shiny lap-top. Normally, when I wrote, I became completely absorbed in whatever story I was telling. Sometimes, hours would pass before a distinct cough or throat-clearing would awaken me, suggesting that I buy something, quickly, to compensate for the space I was taking.

I lived only around the corner in a small, one bedroom apartment. The intimate cafe served well as a setting for my inspiration. It was an inviting little place with its rustic decor: thick, leather-cushioned chairs, large wooden tables and glass, milk-bottle vases, centering them. It was never over-crowded but the faces that *did* enter there, though well blended within my casual awareness, were interesting and diverse. More importantly, though, was the quiet noise - the sounds of books opening and closing, of hot cocoa being poured, of forks clanging against their dishes; of random, whispered voices. They were all a welcome retreat from the silence of my tiny home.

Aside from that, my focus was never really anywhere I was physically. It was always somewhere in the depths of my mind; in a world that nobody could see but me. And it wasn't a lovely world. It wasn't a world I would visit to be free of myself and the life I had chosen. It was a haunting world. It was a world where death lingered long before it came. It was a world where shadows followed and love died. It was a world where all the pain I had ever known lived, quite well, under my care. I needed that world to remain so that I could tell my stories. Because that was all I ever wanted to do.

Before him, it was my only hunger.

On the day I first saw him, I had glanced away from my work in a moment of frustration - perhaps it had been a creative block; perhaps something had distracted me. Whatever the reason, I can't remember. All I know is that I glanced up and there he was, sitting at the table across from me. His hair was black and it flowed past his shoulders in careless, shiny waves. A thin band was wrapped around the top of his head, puffing out the hair above it - but serving its purpose, and keeping any strands from falling into his face. He had thick facial hair - not quite a full-grown beard and mustache, but, in another day or two, it would be - and he wore a simple dark t-shirt, blue jeans and faded leather sandals.

It was easy to see that none of these things were fashion choices - and that he was a person far too intricate for anything one-dimensional. He had been swaying his body - perhaps with every word he typed - as if he were living out his life, straight off the pages in front of him. And his eyes were dark and worn - and so very fierce. They reminded me of a wounded deer I had seen once on a family trip to Pennsylvania. The buck was dying. It had been hit. And I saw, in its eyes, something far greater than that, which I saw in the people I interacted with everyday. I saw life. I saw a being, strong and wild - and running with the others. I saw it fearful in its sprint and the cautioned swaying of its thick, white tail. I saw it peaceful at the water's edge with the ripples glowing beneath the big, hot sun.

I had formed a bond - my first bond. And I told my mother about it. But she shrugged it away, angry that I had wandered off - that I had gotten so close. And she never understood why, for many nights afterward, I cried myself to sleep. She never understood me at all.

"What's your name?" I asked, because I needed to know. But I never moved from my seat.

At first he didn't answer. He wanted to finish typing out his sentence. He wanted to complete his thought. For seconds, I continued to watch his slow, seductive dance. He had found a way to make *sitting* entertaining. When he finally looked up at me he didn't seem surprised that I was addressing him. And he wasn't annoyed at all - as I might have been.

"It's Max," he said. "Short for Maxton."

It fit him. "I'm Brooke," I said.

He nodded. "Your hair is so curly - it just goes in any direction it chooses," he said.

Hmmm. "Yes, I know. For years I've tried to tame it. To no avail. So, I've simply let it be."

He nodded. "I can't imagine it any other way."

I laughed at his brazenness. What right did he have to imagine anything about me? We've only just met!

"You've tried to put highlights in it," he said.

I had forgotten. Many months ago I sprayed a little peroxide in my brown hair to liven it up a little - to bring some intensity to my pale skin. But it had only turned unevenly orange. Now, the color was nearly grown out. "Yes, I suppose."

He scrunched his face up, like a little boy refusing to eat his food. "Don't ever do that again."

I smiled. "I think I've learned my lesson." I gestured toward his laptop. "So, you're a writer. Like me."

He looked at my notebook - surprised that he had failed to miss it. "Interesting," he said, in a long, slow drawl. "Another writer. I've run into many of our kind."

"You sound disappointed," I said.

He smiled. His deep dimples contrasted with his eccentricities. "People tend to disappoint me."

I nodded. "Well then - you can add me to your list."

"Oh? You'll disappoint me?"

"I'm sure of it."

He examined me for a while. He was creating his story of me. He had me all figured out, instantly. "I think you might be right. But - I'd like to know you anyway."

"What do you write?" I asked.

"I write whatever inspires me in the moment. But, that's not always commercially viable."

"True. But who cares."

He groaned. "Unfortunately, I do. I need food on my table."

"Steal scraps," I offered. "Wait tables."

He laughed. It was a nice, deep laugh. "I've had my share of side jobs. Too many to count. Luckily, my royalties help keep me afloat. Because if I depended on those jobs alone I'd be begging you for change right now."

"Oh - have you published something?"

He nodded. "Yes. A thriller. It's quite boring. Made me a little money, though. Nothing too impressive."

I smirked. "Boring? Somehow - I find that hard to believe. Have I heard of it?"

He shrugged. "It's possible." But he didn't go any further into it.

"Please tell me you don't always write long-hand," he

said.

"Yes, yes I do."

"Why? I'm exhausted for you."

"I'm not fast - with the typing."

"Keep trying and you'll get faster."

"I can't learn and write at the same time," I said.

"You're already disappointing me," he said. But he was still smiling. And his eyes were brighter.

"See," I whispered, "I told you."

We encountered each other in that little cafe often after that. Many times we would share the same table, order our respective drinks and write, without talking at all.

It was comforting, being beside him. It was empowering, even. I found that I didn't have many lulls - the words were spilling out of me, easily. I wrote short stories. I wrote beginnings of novels that I would revisit again, soon. I wrote poetry - poetry was always a bit more difficult for me - but I wrote it anyway. Rhyming poetry. Because I liked it. And, in those moments, I would read to him, and our comfortable silence would be broken.

The cobwebs seemed so beautiful
 in their elaborate display
You pulled them from the corners
And I left them, hoping they would stay

"It's haunting," he said, "I'm envisioning an old house - but it's not the house that's depressing - it's them. The two of them. Their love - it's dying. That's what I see. Write this down," he said. And his voice became musical. "The room began to fill with dust, its walls abandoned and alone. We left to search for cleaner air - but couldn't find our way back home."

And he always surprised me. It was like he knew what I needed. He was able to jump out of his own voice - out of his own dark world to join me, in mine; to help me. I didn't have that ability. I had only enough for myself.

Finally, the day came when we packed up our dismal fantasies and walked out the door together, hand in hand. It was a day that brought us to his place by dark. And beneath the tender moonlight glow, we took all of the passion that we gave to our work and poured it onto each other.

He was aggressive and experimental. And his hands didn't leave a part of me untouched. He used scarves and he used candle wax. And beneath his mouth my body jolted against my restraints. We moved, slowly, together, his hair falling into my face - my skin, prickled and ready beneath his firm, warm body. And he pressed into me - my legs wrapping around him, pulling him closer; bringing him deeper.

In the morning I awoke and he wasn't there. There was a note. He had left for work but I should stay as long as I needed to. And then, there was the word - the question. *Love?*

I already knew the answer. But, to see it written in his quick, slanted script drunkened me. It was an amorous, soaring high.

I moved in with him shortly after that. And for months, we lived in blissful content. We would go to our little jobs during the day; meet at the cafe afterwards, then come home and make love way into the morning.

But, we each had demons; and we had pride. We were two creative people living and working together. I had a mother I never connected with, and I was raised without a father. He had wealthy parents - an overly submissive mother and a father who had disowned him when he failed to enter the family business. We hadn't gotten over the disjointed relationships of our past. Wasn't that a recipe for disaster?

We started fighting - about everything.

"You're never going to finish - you need a laptop," he

would say.

"I don't want one."

"You've been working on that book since I met you - you haven't gotten far at all."

"I don't care - what's the rush? I'm not in a rush."

"I thought you had bigger dreams."

"No," I would say, irritated, "That's you - not me."

"How can you be content like this?"

"I'm not! Not with you bossing me around all the time!" And I would slam the bedroom door, and he would sleep on the couch.

Some days it was my fault.

"We're out of toilet paper again! Why didn't you pick any up?" I would say.

And he would move slowly across the room. He did many things slowly. It irritated me. "It's *my* job to get toilet paper?"

"Yes! Because I do everything! I shop. I clean. I cook! All you do is write. I'm fucking tired of it!"

And his face would become red and his eyes would be fiery. "I work two jobs, sometimes three - so that you can survive on your part time job - so that you can have more than that twin bedroom you lived in!"

"I didn't ask for this!"

"Yes you did! Not with words - but you asked for it!"

And I would groan. "Stop it! Just stop it! Not everything is poetry - not everything's a metaphor! Sometimes I say what I mean and mean what I say! Goddammit!"

They were silly arguments. Stupid fights. And always, one of us would end up apologizing. And we would fall into bed together - because there, neither of us would be judged Naked, we were open and honest, seductive and unarmed - and any anger looming would be nourished within our animalistic fornication.

I wrote many entries in my journal. It was a book that I started when I met him. It was a book that would be our fascinating love story one day.

January 10

I can do anything in Maxton's eyes. It's a lot of pressure, though. He sees so much in me. I don't share his vision. And he hates me for it.

March 19

Max finished his second novel. I read it. It surpassed anything I could have ever imagined. It's true literature. His publisher despises it. They tell him nobody will understand it. Max has been sulking. His publisher is right. But what does it matter?

May 11

Max fucked me all day. I woke up to breakfast in bed — cereal, bacon and warm biscuits. We ate together, then he tied me to the bed post. Later, I blindfolded him and poured ice on his body. He tried to move but I had him tightly bound. I watched as the ice melted, slowly. It was a seductive experience. I watched his chest move up and down beneath the ice. I watched the cubes get smaller, and the water running down the sides of his skin. I watched and I waited until there was nothing left but him, heated and damp. Then I got on top.

August 5

I finally finished my first book. It's a story about a woman in love with someone else's shadow. It's less complicated than it sounds. It's more about self-discovery. Max has edited it for me. He tells me it's wonderful. He tells me he will give it to his publisher. I know he has high hopes for me. But he's a better writer than I am. We both know it.

September 10

Max asked me to marry him.

I hadn't been expecting it at all. Max had come home one evening - later than usual. I was reading the poem I had written at the cafe - the one about the house of webs. I wanted to finish it but I couldn't find the words past what he had added.

> The cobwebs seemed so beautiful
> in their elaborate display
> You pulled them from the corners
> And I left them, hoping they would stay
>
> The room began to fill with dust
> Its walls, abandoned and alone
> We left to search for cleaner air
> But couldn't find our way back home

I was sitting in his favorite green chair. I had a checkered, brown fleece blanket covering me. It was beginning to get cold outside. My hair was piled on top of my head, sprouting up in thick, wiry springs. I was tired. But I was cozy.

He walked through the door. His face, for the first time, was clean-shaven and shiny. His thick hair was pulled back into a loose pony-tail. He looked younger, in that moment. I realized just how handsome he really was. He had a face that could be found on the cover of a magazine. He was beautiful.

"Wow," I said, as he planted a soft, smooth kiss on my lips. For a moment, he lingered there - his sweet breath, warm against my mouth. "I can't believe your face." I touched his skin. It was creamy. He hated that he was handsome. He hated being judged on anything, other than his work.

"Surprised?" he asked.

I nodded. "I didn't think I would like you without facial hair. I've become so accustomed to it." And I winked at him. "But, I like it. It's like I'm with a different man. It's kinda exciting."

He laughed. He smelled of trees and of long, wet grass. It was like the outside breeze on a fall morning, right after a rainstorm.

He kissed me again and I slipped my arms around his neck. "Take me. Right here," I said.

He moaned. "Soon," he said. "I want to talk to you."

I sat up. "Uh-oh."

"No - it's nothing to worry about. It's - I don't think, at least."

"What is it?"

He took a deep breath. He pulled a brown box out of his inner jacket pocket.

Even then it didn't hit me.

"It's been a wild year," he said. Then, he chuckled. "I mean - I go to a coffee shop, to write - to be one, with myself, and there's a girl there - a strange-looking, skinny girl, with big, crazy hair. I mean, this girl looked like she just got electric-shocked."

"Thanks," I said, smiling. "Stop talking about me

in the third person."

Ignoring my request, he continued. "And she's talking to me. Out of nowhere. She just assumed I would to talk to her."

I giggled. "Of course. I'm interesting."

His eyelids lowered and he smiled. "You are. Very interesting. I can honestly say you've disappointed me the least."

"Ha!" I said, playfully smacking him. "I think that's the best compliment I've ever received."

His face got serious. "It hasn't always been easy," he said, "Man - you have a temper on you. You really do. I think I've spent way too many nights on the couch."

"Oh stop. I've never let you spend an entire night on the couch. I always make it better. I always wake you up." And I wriggled my body against his.

"Yes, you have." He ran his fingers against my thigh. "You certainly know how to wake me up." And for a moment, we were lost in our bliss. Then, he spoke again. "But, I think we work because we really want it to work. We know it's worth it."

"We *are* worth it, Maxton," I said.

He sighed. "I hate when you call me that."

I stroked his cheek. It was hard not to touch his face. "And I hate when you make fun of my hair."

"Marry me," he said.

And my eyes widened. "What?" I laughed. Then, I was silent.

"Marry me, Brooke. You have to. We're in love."

I wanted to marry him. There was nothing I've ever wanted more in my entire life. I felt my hands beginning to tremble. He squeezed them. He kissed them.

"Yes, Max. Yes - I want to marry you. What - how long did you plan this for? I'm so - I'm speechless."

He opened the box and in it there was a small, silver ring with a green, tourmaline stone. It was my birthstone. It was beautiful.

He slipped it onto my finger. It was a little big but it didn't matter. It symbolized so many things. To me, it was a symbol of rebirth, of change - of deep, chaotic love. I pulled my hand, protectively, to my heart. "It's perfect." I felt the tears streaming down my cheeks. "Why'd you have to go and make me cry," I said.

He smiled and stood up. He reached his hand out to me. "Come into the bedroom?"

I nodded.

That night, we made love. We cried as we held each other. We kissed, naked and intertwined, for many minutes - our lips, soft and slow in our rediscovery. We were gentle and we were patient. We were washing away our pasts. We were entering a new chapter.

We decided we would elope. But we would wait. We would wait until the spring – so we could be amongst the flowers. I would wear a simple, white summer dress. He would wear beige linen.

We talked about the years ahead of us. We talked about writing a book together. We talked about the children we would have. They would be writers, like us. They would be interesting and unique. And we would love them. And we would know them. There would be no skeletons in their closets; no childhood relationships they would have to overcome.

"We'll buy a house on a lake," Max said, "And we'll get a pontoon."

"Oooh, that sounds nice. Can we float, naked, under the sun?"

"Yes," Max said, "but, we'll probably get shot for doing it."

"Oh – you're ruining my fantasy! Don't bring violence into it."

Max laughed. "Okay, can I rewind?"

"Yes. Go again."

"Okay – so, we'll buy a house by the river," he said.

"I'm listening. Can we get a pontoon?"

"We'll get a rowboat. And – we can row, naked. Because everyone around us will be naked, too."

I scrunched my nose. "Honey - maybe I should do this. I don't want a bunch of weird, naked people in my fantasy!"

"Okay – you go."

I smiled, slithering close to him. "We'll buy a cabin in the woods. And, we'll have nobody anywhere near us. Only the animals. And the mountains will be in the distance – we'll see them, easily, every morning, while we're drinking our coffee on the porch. And in the evenings, we'll have sex in front of a large, roaring fire. And we'll buy thick, animal-print quilts. And we'll make fresh lemonade."

Max nodded. "That's very tempting. Very."

I giggled.

He kissed my forehead. "You, my love, are an amazing story teller. Better than you realize."

"Thanks."

"I would lose the lemonade part, though."

I shoved him. "What?!"

"Well," he said, "I was thinking – *winter*. Cold, wet snow. Roaring fire. The lemonade – it through me off."

I shook my head, sighing. "You're a piece of work."

"I'll take that as a compliment," he said.

"People *do* drink lemonade in the winter."

He shook his head. "Not in our fantasy."

October 31,
There was an accident.

They say when something so shocking occurs, your body goes into defense mode. It protects you. Isn't that ironic? It protects you after the unimaginable already happens. They say you go through a series of emotions. Sometimes, you don't feel anything at all. Sometimes, you retreat somewhere inside yourself.

I wasn't that lucky.

Max's car had been hit by a drunk driver. It was a truck full of teenagers. It was Halloween. It was a night when many people celebrated. Sometimes, they drank too much. Nobody died. The kids - they were bruised. They were sorry. And – eventually, they would pay. Justice would be served. At least in the eyes of the law.

For Max, it was impossible for justice to be served. His car had tumbled down a hill - *like a matchbox car*, he said. Like a crumpled toy. And he was ejected from his seat, hitting his head and twisting his spine.

The doctor said he suffered a severe injury to his nerves. They called it an 'incomplete spinal cord injury'. He would be paralyzed from the waist down. One of his arms had lost most of its function.

He would have to go through rehabilitation. He would have to go home, to his father.

"What? That's silly, Max. I can take care of you. You're going to be okay," I had said, weeks after the accident. I was standing above his hospital bed, running my fingers against his swollen, bruised face. His hair had been partially shaved. He was disappearing.

"It's too much. You can't. We don't have the means," he said.

"I'm going to be your wife, Max - we'll have to figure it out."

He didn't reply. He looked away. His lip was trembling.

"Shhh," I whispered, putting my hand into his. But his fingers remained limp. He didn't even know I was touching him.

I stayed with him every night. I went home, only to shower. I stopped writing. I stopped living. My mind was racing - my energy was overflowing, for him.

I thought about our future together. It was suddenly dim. I thought about the man I had met in the cafe. I thought about the hands that may never type again. I thought about the legs that may never walk again. I thought about us and everything we were about. I looked at the green gemstone on my finger and I kissed it, many times. I made silent wishes. I hoped something magical would happen. I was angry. I was sorry for him.

I was sorry for me.

I would sleep only in twenty-minute intervals - and only when I knew Maxton was asleep. And I would dream of him, energetic and in motion on top of me. I would be able to taste his sweat. I would be able to join, easily, in his laughter - because it was full-bodied; because it was life. And always, before I awoke, I was brought back to the woods, off that Pennsylvania highway - where the deer lay breathing in slow, shallow gasps; where it was watching me.

When I received the phone call from Maxton's publishing house, I was barely coherent.

"What?" I had said. It was only a jumbled pile of words I was hearing. It was a voice - a bland, repetitive sound, possibly feigning excitement.

"We want to work with you," he was saying.

"Work with me?"

"We want to publish your work. We think you have a real voice."

And I had been washing Maxton's undershirts. I had been packing a bag for him. He needed things. "Oh," I said, disinterested. "You liked my book? I forgot," I said, my voice barely audible. "I forgot Max had sent it."

The man was silent for a moment. "I'm sorry about Max," he said.

"He's not dead," I said, rather abruptly. Then, I sighed. I was being rude. I was taking my anger out on a stranger. He didn't say he was dead. He said he was sorry. He was sorry that Max had become only a shadow of the man he used to be. And not just in the physical sense.

"I'm sorry," I said. "I haven't been sleeping much. Thank you."

The man cleared his throat. "I know you have a lot on your plate right now. So, take what I'm saying and sit with it for a while."

I nodded. To myself. "Okay."

"Max sent me your journal."

I was confused. My journal? Then, a jolt of energy spiked through me. "What?" And suddenly, I was vividly awake.

I dropped the phone and ran into the bedroom. I threw my body against the nightstand, yanking open the drawer – causing it to come off the hinges and fall onto the floor. I rummaged, frantically, through the papers, throwing them behind me.

My journal was gone. But hadn't I known this? Hadn't I looked for it more than once? Hadn't I shrugged it off thinking I had thrown it in another drawer?

No! My screams echoed through the apartment. I savagely ripped at my hair. *What the fuck?!*

I curled my body into a ball on the floor beside my bed. I felt raped.

When, finally, I gained my composure, I walked over to the phone. I picked it up. I heard the man breathing. He hadn't disconnected the line.

"Brooke?" he asked. "Are you okay?"

I stayed silent.

"He told me you knew," the man said.

I shook my head, tasting my salty tears. "No he didn't."

The man cleared his throat again. "You have a great story. And your writing - it's unsparing."

What the fuck did that even mean? I shook my head, even though he couldn't see me. "This is not my writing," I said, "It's personal – it's a journal. You know, like a diary. It's not a novel. It's not for sale."

"It can be something great," the man said. "I have ideas."

I didn't respond.

"Think about what I'm saying, Brooke."

Later, when Max awoke, I was sitting across from him. I had come, angry. I was prepared to fight. But, watching him sleep - seemingly small and frail; his eyelids twitching with whatever nightmare he was having - seeped the anger right out of me.

"You've been naughty," I said.

He squinted. "What?"

"Your publisher called me."

His eyes widened and I saw a smile spreading across his lips. He had not smiled once since the accident. "They liked it?"

"They liked what?" I asked.

He took in a deep breath. It was a struggle for him. "You have every right to be mad. I shouldn't have given it to him. I shouldn't have read it."

"Why did you?" I asked.

He looked at me, long and hard. "Because I knew you had it in you. Because I wanted to find your voice."

"So - it was a crock of shit? Everything you said about my other book? Did you even send it?"

He nodded. "I did. They didn't like it."

I raised my eyebrows. "Really."

"Really. Because you were holding back. I didn't want to discourage you so I didn't tell you."

I shook my head and looked at the ceiling. There was a long crack running across it. "So that gave you the right to read my journal?"

"No," he said. "But once I did, I knew you deserved more." Then, a chuckle erupted from his lips. "It was about *us*, Brooke. It was about *me* – all of my ridiculous idiosyncrasies. Who would've thought I was that compelling? Not me. It was difficult to read, at times. But at the same time, easy." He looked at me. "It was good, Brooke. Raw."

"Of course it was raw. Because nobody else was supposed to read it! Those were my secrets. Mine," I said.

"Oh, Brooke – you always said that you would turn it into a book, one day. Didn't you?"

I stood. "Yes - one day. And - I wasn't planning on submitting my entire journal. I mean - I would have edited it. My God, Maxton - I wrote details about our sex life!"

"You would have edited out the meat."

I nodded. "Maybe. But - that would have been my decision."

I sat back down. The color that had momentarily filled Maxton's face was draining. Our conversation had weakened him.

"You'll thank me, one day," he said. Then, before I could reply. "I'm going home."

My eyes widened. "When?"

He sighed. "Not to our home. I'm going home - my childhood home. My dad is here. He's in with the doctor now. There will be a better set up for me there."

I felt the knife, cold and sharp against my skin. "What do you mean, Max? Your home is with me."

I saw the struggle in his face. He wanted to burst out his emotions – but his body wouldn't let him. "Brooke," he said, his voice urgent, "we're not going to be able to have sex. I mean, God, Brooke - I can't fucking get hard."

I shrugged. "So what? What the fuck? What do you think marriage is about? I'm just supposed to let you leave?"

"That's the thing, Brooke. We're not married yet."

I stared at the ring. It was dull against the fluorescent lights. I felt the draining of my energy - of my world. "Max," I whispered, "Please don't say anymore." I was pleading with him. The tears were blinding me. "I love you. We love each other." What was my life without him? His mind was still here – his brilliant, beautiful mind. And – he was able to move, a little. The doctor said there was a good possibility that he could improve a lot more with time.

"That will change."

"How can you say that?" And I didn't care that my voice had risen. I didn't care that my tears were now spilling off my face and onto my thin, cotton shirt.

"Shhh. Lower your voice. They're going to make you leave," he said.

"I'm not letting you go," I said.

"You don't have a choice, Brooke." And this time, his voice was strong - stronger than he looked. "I need to be a child again for a while. I need to be really ugly right now. I can't be that with you. I don't want you to see me like that."

"You'll never be ugly to me, Maxton. Don't you know that?"

He closed his eyes, slowly. For a long while, he didn't speak. I thought maybe he had fallen asleep. I thought maybe I had won the battle.

"Brooke," he whispered, his eyes still closed. "I want you to keep the ring. I want you to stay at the apartment. I'm going to arrange to have it paid off - for a year."

I thought about his father. I thought about all the money he had grown up with. He had given it all up; he had walked away from it to write, to live, simply. To meet me.

He was getting upset. He didn't want me to fight him. "I don't want you to do that," I said, softly, feeling defeated. I wanted to scream at him. I wanted to tell him he was a fucking coward! I wanted to tell him that he was more than just a fucking body! I loved him for everything he was, inside. He was a master of sentences, he was convoluted and broken, but he didn't care – he didn't harp on it. He took the ordinary and made it extraordinary – from the very first day. And none of this had been taken from him. The most important part of who he was, remained.

But I said none of that. "I can manage," I said, instead. Because that is what he wanted me to say.

"Let them publish your journal. They'll edit it - you'll be happy in the end. I promise."

I didn't say anything.

"I don't want to say goodbye to you, Brooke." He was like a child trying not to cry. "I just can't. It's too final, you know? And who knows where we'll be next year, right?"

I saw the lone tear trailing its way down his cheek and onto the pillow.

I walked over to him and put my hand on his face. His eyes were pink. His bruises were fading. I bent down and kissed him on the lips, savoring, for many moments, his sweet, stale breath.

"You were," I said, trying to keep things light – but wanting so much to say something effective, "My least disappointment."

And he tried to laugh, but something in his throat stopped him. "And," he said, choking on his words. "You were mine."

Later that evening, when the curtains were drawn, and the brown, checkered blanket was draped upon me, I inspected every inch of our apartment.

There wasn't a corner that didn't have a memory. There wasn't a spot where I didn't see us fighting, or laughing - or naked and loving each other.

I wouldn't stay there. I couldn't.

I twisted the ring on my finger. It was sparkling now, away from the dreary hospital glare. It was pretty.

Pretty. What was pretty?

I closed my eyes. I was back in Pennsylvania, amongst the tall, winding trees. I heard the cars - somewhere nearby. The buck's breathing was barely audible. He was watching me. He was speaking to me. He wasn't scared anymore. I didn't want to leave him. I knew my mother was looking for me, but I didn't care. I stayed with him - for long, intimate moments until he took his final breath. *You'll be okay*, I whispered. *You're going to a better place*. And when, finally, he was still, his eyes remained open. But the story they told had disappeared.

I would keep the ring. Forever.

I picked up an old, yellow notebook. I opened to the first page. There was some scribbling – some numbers written down; a bill we hadn't yet paid. It was insignificant. It was unimportant nonsense.

But it was him. It was his handwriting. It was from a time when he could move a pen, easily. It was from a time when our greatest problem was a high electric bill – or a roll of toilet paper that had been forgotten.

I turned to the next page. It was blank. It was waiting for me.

> The cobwebs seemed so beautiful
> in their elaborate display
> You pulled them from the corners
> And I left them, hoping they would stay
>
> The room began to fill with dust
> Its walls abandoned and alone
> We left to search for cleaner air
> But couldn't find our way back home
>
> The hours seem to disarrange
> Like words that cannot form a thought
> They sit there on an empty stage
> With all the silence we have brought

And everything around me seems to move a
little slow
And you are found, upside down, everywhere I
go
And I am not seduced by all the splendor of this
place
For all I see are shadows, and the footprints, and
the space

3 AN INCREDIBLY DISMAL SATURDAY

The sun is burning my eyes. I try to tell you but I don't know how. I shut my eyes and keep them shut for a long, long time. Maybe I fall asleep. When I open them, it's not bright anymore. And we have stopped moving. You are standing outside. You are stretching. You don't care that your hair is getting damp. You turn to look at me. You run your hands across the window, wiping the rain away. For a moment, you are distracted and your eyes leave me - but your hand stays on the glass. Your floral dress is billowing, and because of this, I want to touch you. But I can't. Instead, I place my hand against the window so it looks like we are touching. We stay like this for a while. When you move, there is an imprint where your hand had been. I like that you have left something behind. But, soon, it is distorted by the rain - and I watch as your fingers disappear.

You are in the car again and we are moving. There is music - a song that sounds familiar. I feel my lips trying to form the words. I have almost found them - I am almost there. But you beat me to it. You start to sing. I laugh, because you sound funny - and because of the way you are swaying back and forth in your seat. Then, you roll up your window and I smell something; something rancid. It's the food in the crumpled bag, peeking from beneath the seat. I want to tell you it's there. I point. I throw my squishy doll at you. You are still singing. The window – no, past the window, everything is moving so quickly, the trees, the buildings, the people, hurrying to get out of the rain. You turn to me; your curled, yellow hair is pinned back, away from your face. Your eyes are wide and they are very blue now. You are smiling at me. You are blowing me a kiss. We connect. We are one. I want you to crawl back here, with me, so we can watch the world as it rushes past us.

I won the spelling bee. The trophy is shiny and golden. I think it is the biggest thing in the world to ever happen and I can't wait to tell you. I run home, the squirrels racing ahead of me, making a path – just so I can get to you; just so I can show you. The neighbor next door is outside, in front of his house. He is standing with his hands in his pockets. He is hunched over and his skin is crinkled. I wave but he doesn't wave back. I think he wants to drink me. I think he wants to sip the energy right out of me. For a moment, when I pass him, my movements become slow. But, then, like a magnet, I am pulled quickly toward the big red doors - because you are somewhere behind them. When I enter, I realize that *they* are here – all the ones who make me, me; the man with the books, the man with the guitar – the women with their grudges and their heavy backpacks. They all love me, kind of - at least I think so. But some of them will prove me wrong.

You are there with your blue pants and wide hips. You are pretending to smoke a cigarette. Because *they* like to smoke. You are standing over the kitchen counter making sure there is enough food for everyone. *He* is there, too. Our strength. Your everything. And he is brushing the hair out of your face. I tell you, *I've won* –

Look, I've won! And they all begin to laugh at me. Their faces are like carnival clowns. Did you steal that? they ask. But I didn't. I laugh with them, but I tell you with my eyes – *I didn't steal it! I won it.* And you are looking at him. You are smiling. *I didn't steal it. I won it. It's a prize.* But you join in with them - you are laughing, now, too. And so is he. You never tell me you are joking.

We are in a motel room in Connecticut. I am jumping on the bed. You are fighting with him. We are supposed to be somewhere else – but you have changed your mind; you don't want to go now. *They* won't understand, you are saying. And he is angry – he is angry, because we have come all this way. But he doesn't raise his voice. I know he is mad, only because of the way his cheeks tighten. You are yelling. You always yell. Because if you don't he might not understand you. I keep jumping on the bed. I am in my red, velvet dress. You have put my hair in pigtails – and you have wrapped them in silky, white ribbon. I am your prize; the one reflected in your eyes. We will stay the night – because we have driven three hours. We will go back in the morning. We came for nothing. We came so I can jump on the bed. We came so you can yell without our neighbors hearing.

I haven't seen them in many, many days. They are mentioned only in scattered sentences that I'm not supposed to hear. The world has become quiet - so quiet, it's as if I have forgotten the horse shoe games, and the way we huddled in large, sandy bunches by the water. Now, it's just you and him. And me. Sometimes we sit around the table and say nothing at all. Sometimes, I ask questions - like the show on television. I ask both of you, separately, to see if your answers match. They always do. Because you know each other. *Like a pair of old socks*, he says. You don't like that. And you have stopped looking at him. And he has stopped brushing the hair out of your face.

I am playing ball – but the woman with the black hair yells at me. She yells, because the ball is in her flower garden again. It is nothing. It is like a loud, annoying bird that will eventually go away. But, you make it something. You are mad - you are so mad, because, how dare she yell at me? You come outside. You are in front of her, pointing in her face. I run inside. I peek out the window. You are like a raging fire.

They have arrived. They smell like wet, black snow. They are brushing themselves off. They are hanging their coats. They don't hug him, or you. But they hug me. I am happy to see them. I have so much to tell them. But, they are whispering in the corners. They are talking about him. *Too skinny*, they say. I want to see the fireworks. I want to go to the fair. Nobody takes me.

He wants to see her. He says she held me when I was a baby. He says there are things that must be said. We go together - with you. He tells us to wait in the car. But I don't. I follow him up the long, curved staircase. Everything is dusty. She answers the door. She is withered and small. And she is empty, in the eyes. She doesn't know him anymore. She is frightened. She calls him a monster, and she howls until we leave. I am quick - I am desperate to get to you. But he is dragging. He is looking back for her. We drive for a block then he pulls the car over. You are asking him, *What?* Then, he vomits out the window. You are worried. *Should we go to the hospital?* you ask. But he shakes his head. He is crying. I see the tears every time the street light shines on his face. It is a long ride home.

I am in my bed but I can't sleep because you are fighting with him. He tells you that you must learn. He tells you that you must try. But you refuse. You don't need to. You say that he is getting ahead of himself. He is angry - so angry that he packs his bag and slams the front door behind him. You tell him, *Good! Go, and don't come back*! But you stay at the window for the whole fifteen minutes. You need him. I know it. And he comes back. Because he is too tired to walk around the block any longer.

They say he looks ugly. Why do they say that? He looks the same. He is tall, still, and handsome - like the man in the black and white film. So what if he has shadows under his eyes? So what if his belly isn't round anymore? I am mad at them. They are different. They are like dark corners in an old, abandoned house. He is not one of them, anymore. We all know it. So I don't know why he goes with them. He is gone for days. Sometimes you leave me to go see him. When he comes back, you hug him for a long, long time. Then, you put him to bed. *Can I sleep with him*? I ask. You say no.

I need him to help me with my homework. He is watching the news. He is sitting in his flannel pajamas. His black hair is thinning, just like his face. *Can you do this*? I ask. I have to draw a straight line. He is glad that I need him. He tries to help me. He draws the line but it's not so straight. I thank him. I kiss him on the cheek. I tell him it's perfect. When he's not looking, I crumple it up and throw it away. I sneak into the other room - where you are sitting; where you are holding the ugly, green phone. I ask you to draw it again. You do it. Perfectly. Even though I have only half of your attention. He catches us. He makes a sad face because I didn't like his drawing. He never tells me he is joking.

I open my eyes. I sit up. Something has startled me. Something has happened. The blackness becomes less black, because the light is seeping in from beneath the bedroom door. You are in another room - you are saying something. No - you are yelling. You are telling me to wake up - to get out of bed. I don't understand. Why? I hear you screaming, *Come quickly*! I don't move. I pull the covers over me and curl into a ball. Soon, the lights are swirling around outside my window. I hear people - I hear talking, but I don't know what they say. When it is quiet again, I get out of bed. I tiptoe into the living room, but a stranger is there — the woman, next door, with the white cat. You have gone with him. She will spend the night.

He doesn't come home with you. You are sitting on the chair by the window. You are looking out. Your eyes are droopy. I look out, too. But there is nothing there. Only the empty trees with the black, snaky arms. I pull at your sleeve but you are like a statue.

I am in the long hallway with the crisp, shiny floors. I miss him. I want to see him. I tell you this but you say no. I'm too young. The people in white won't let me. *I tried*, you say, *I know it's important.* I stand outside the door, alone. The people are rolling out his empty bed. He had an accident. Everything's all wet! They are laughing at him. They don't see me. When they are gone, you take me outside - to the window. Because he is on the ground floor. We squeeze through the bushes until I am pressed up against the brick. *Look*, you say. And I stand on my tip-toes. I see him, pale and faded, past the frosty glass. He waves to me. I wave back. Then, you send me home with someone else.

They have come again. They are sitting in my bedroom, with their squinty, sorry eyes. He is gone. That's what they are telling me. *Gone?* I ask. *He is always gone.* They say this time it's different. They say this time he won't be coming back. I look at you - because I want

you to hear what's in my mind. But, you don't hear me.
Because you are not listening. You are crying. And they
are holding you up because you can't hold yourself up. I
want to cry, too, because I didn't keep his drawing. I want
to cry, too, because I didn't kiss the frosty glass. But I
think you are crying for us both. So, I don't do anything at
all.

Your shadow has changed. I trace it with my
finger. It's easy to do because you're always so still now.
You are sitting at the table. The papers are all around you.
Your head is in your hands. *What's wrong?* I ask. You look
at me. You forgot I was next to you. *Somebody will be living
here,* you say, *Someone we don't know. Because we need the money.*
I tell you I don't mind.

You don't smile so much anymore. Even when I
tell you a joke. But you are suddenly quicker with
numbers. And you've learned how to mow the lawn.
When you come inside there is dirt on your face. And I
reach for you - to wipe it away. But you stop me. You
won't let me touch you.

They have not returned. You are tired, so it's okay.
They were never yours, anyway. At least that's what you
mumble. The woman in the picture is here. She is helping
you with me. She puts a skinny tree up, in the corner.
That's not where it goes, I say. But she doesn't listen. She
puts it there anyway. And soon, it is lit - but it doesn't
light the room. You don't want to look at it. And they
don't come to make it pretty like they used to.

You are crying on the couch. I make the music
louder. It is so loud but I can't get the sound of you out of
my head. You cry so much I don't see the tears anymore.
She thinks I am bad. Maybe I am.

You need your pajamas on. She is not here. You ask me to change you. Why? Why can't you change yourself? I pull your t-shirt up above your head. It smells. You are naked. You have marks on your skin. Your bones - I can see them. Your breasts - they are lifeless. I put the pink night-dress over your head and pull it down – to cover you. I need to cover you. The last time you wore it, you were flipping pancakes in the kitchen and your legs were thick and strong. And he was laughing, behind you. When I am finished, you thank me. But your voice is so low I can barely hear it. I leave the room and close the door behind me.

You are quiet. You don't cry anymore. You are in your bed, sleeping – always sleeping. She is here all the time now. Because I need someone to take care of me. She speaks about you as if you are someone else. She says you were different. She says you wanted more. And now look. Now look where you are. She's talking in riddles. I don't understand. I hate this. I want to push past her to get to you. Where did you go? Even when I'm next to you, I'm not with you at all.

They are back. They are whispering again. They are walking through the rooms pointing at things, wanting to make change. You are not here. Somebody has taken you. Like him, you have disappeared. I look - and you are not found. I don't like it. I want you. I tell them I want you. They gather around me like a thick, winter coat. They understand.

They take me to you. This time, the people in white let me see you. This time, it's okay. Maybe because it's lunchtime. Maybe because it's Saturday. I don't know. And I don't ask. Because I can't stop looking at you. You don't look like you at all. Your skin looks like paper. Your head is tilted to the side. You cannot move. You cannot speak. I hold my breath and I imagine that I am underwater. Because that is where I see you instead of tangled in these tubes. Why are there so many? Can you hear me, now, at all? Your eyes are darting all around the room. Then, they find me and they settle into mine. I see a tear running down your face. Your cheek is hollow and dark. I want to hug you. I want to be back in the car with the rancid smell - because then, it was only food - and your skin was shimmering - and the world moved hastily around us because every moment was only ours. I want to tell you something very simple. I want to tell you that I love you. But, I don't know how to say it. And they are hurrying me out. They are telling me to say goodbye. But I won't. Instead, I blow you a kiss.

I go outside. I wait on the steps in front of the big, cold building. Everything is cold. Everything is blue. I look up. I try to find your window. But, I can't see. Because the sun is burning my eyes.

4 BAREFOOT IN THE PEA GREEN POND

Today you asked me why I loved my father. It wasn't an odd question. It wasn't a question I hadn't asked myself before. But you wanted an answer immediately. *Is it out of obligation? Is it because he's your dad?* I wanted to form the words but nothing that began could be finished with the truth. Because the truth had not yet been found.

You, with your shiny, ginger hair - your green, feline eyes and milky skin; what did you know of imperfection? You saw me, tall and successful - you envisioned drippings of hard-earned money decorating your skin. You wanted me. You wanted all of me, you said. And you got me. And it was lovely - our trips to Venice, though I preferred less touristy travels - our nights, leaving the opera, the fervor burning in your eyes because they whispered and they wanted but they couldn't have; the silk, falling off your body. Yes, I was quite possessed. So much so, that I needed to bring you home.

And so we went, leaving the lights of the city behind us and the homes turned to trees and the roads turned to dirt. And you, with your stainless, creamy cashmere, were quiet - but your eyes were everywhere.

What is it? I had asked.

You shrugged. *Nothing. It's so desolate.*

I laughed. I tried to loosen the air around us. *It's just for a weekend. You'll survive.*

And you laughed, too - but it was feigned. You were being a sport. Of course you'd survive! But your fingers loosened their grip around mine. And I knew it wouldn't be the first time.

We arrived just before midnight. We pulled up to the small cape with its cedar vinyl exterior. *It used to be log,* I said. You didn't reply. You were looking around at the darkness - at the hovering, black branches - at the full, bright moon in the distance. I was looking at the light flickering in the window.

Together, we walked toward the door - the silent sounds filling up our ears. You pressed your body close to me. *Hurry,* you whispered. You were scared. You weren't used to it. You were used to the beautiful city filth. The freshness, here, was stifling to you.

I saw visions of muddy bicycles cutting through the grass. I saw him, sitting beside me amongst the reeds and cattails, our fishing lines, motionless, in the pea-green pond. I saw, me, on the bulldozer, riding in circles beneath the big, hot sun.

I didn't need to knock. I knew it would be open. Once inside, the stale, musty fragrance engulfed us. You put your hand to your nose. You would get used to it.

He was snoring, in his favorite green recliner - the yellow stuffing seeping through the rips. His white t-shirt was discolored in scattered spots across his chest, and his jeans were tight against his belly. His thick hair, once dark, was white, now. And so was the stubble creeping around his open mouth.

Meet my father.

He's asleep, you said, as if it weren't obvious.

I walked over to the candle and blew it out. The

light from the kitchen was enough, now. *What do you expect?* I asked. *It's midnight.*

You chuckled, nervously.

Come, lets go to sleep, I said.

I brought you to the room in the back. The room that used to be mine. I removed the thinning sheets from the twin bed and replaced them with the crisp, white ones I had purchased on the way. You changed into your red, satin pajamas. You pulled your hair out of the clip. I looked at you - your nipples peeking through the fabric, your hair flowing around the curves of your soft face. Oh, how I wanted to make love to you right there. Oh, how I longed to throw you onto the gloomy bed - the bed with all its heavy weight. For then, wouldn't it be cleansed? Didn't you, with your delicate contours and sweet porcelain skin, have the ability to erase all that it held?

But you were in no mood for that. Your eyes told me exactly what I expected them to say. Too much, too soon.

The bed was too small for the both of us. *Try to sleep*, I said, *I'll be on the couch.*

In the morning he was up before us making pancakes. I heard him in the kitchen and so I rose - to greet him. I went to kiss his cheek but he backed away and extended his hand. I shook it, and my grip was as firm as he wanted it to be. It was all coming back to me now.

He had showered. His hair was damp. And he was wearing cheap cologne. But he still wore the yellowing t-shirt.

Who's the girl? he asked. He had no need for small talk.

She's mine, I said, as if you were a possession. Because I knew that was how he would see you.

Then, you came out, warming the fluorescent room. *Hello*, you said, in your sweetest melody. And he nodded, grumbling.

You looked at me, questioningly. I shrugged.

Later, when we were sitting on the cold, blue kitchen chairs - your feet, already carrying the dirt - he was laughing. He had told a joke - the one about the niggers. Your face was becoming distorted and you were shuffling in your seat. The disapproval set like stones in your eyes. But he wouldn't notice. And he would keep telling his jokes until one of us laughed.

By noon, he was drunk and his words were coming out in drooled, incoherent phrases. The laughing had stopped. I asked if you wanted to take a walk. There was a trail, not far away. You jumped at the chance to get out - to get away from the vile being that raised me. When we were pushing through the branches and the small cedar cape was nowhere to be found, you spoke.

Does he always drink so early? And I thought it was a good way to begin.

Yes.

You sighed, not sure if you should say more.

Go on, I insisted. I wanted you to get it out.

He's just so different - from you.

I nodded. *Yup. But - this is where I came from.*

Was he like this when you were little?

I thought of the time I stood at the window waiting to see the reindeer fly. I was certain that, this time, they would appear - and they would move, magically, before me in strong, sparkling motion.

Instead, the shadow loomed behind me, and I was startled because it darkened the room. *I couldn't sleep*, I said. And he had been angry. *Do reindeer fly?* he asked. And I nodded, slowly. The shadow moved closer. *Do reindeer fly?* he asked, again. This time his voice was urgent. I nodded. Now he was in front of me, his face, sallow against the moonlight - his eyes, black. *Do reindeer fly?* he asked. I knew what he wanted me to say. But I didn't want to say it. I nodded. And then, I saw nothing.

Yes, I told you, *he was always like this.*

You shuddered. *What about your mother?*

Perhaps I should have told you more about me. Perhaps it was silly to let you believe I came from bigger, better things. But I liked the way I looked in your eyes.

She died. I don't remember much about her. Only that she smelled clean - like you. And her fingernails were pink.

Your eyes lowered. You were sorry for me. I bit my lip. I tasted the blood.

I think maybe we should leave this evening, you said. *What do you think?*

I sighed. *Why leave?* Not that I didn't know. Because I did. You weren't comfortable. Why stay, when our host was belligerent and drunk? Why sleep in an uncomfortable bed, in a dark, dingy room, in a dirty, old house that smelled of sweat and rotten food? Why - when I had a crisp, shiny Park Avenue home with a twinkling view of the city?

Because, for all of my childhood this was the place I called home. It was more a part of me than Manhattan would ever be. And you needed to experience it. I needed you to.

I don't know. I mean - you actually want to stay?

I nodded.

You want to stay with your dad, here?

I nodded. Were you going to ask me a third time?

But instead, you changed the question. *Why do you love him?* And you asked it so innocently, so sincerely, that I wanted to strip away your designer dress - which wasn't at all appropriate for where we were - and leave you, naked and lost, here in the middle of the forest.

I walked and you followed. Then, we found a log and sat on it.

It's impossible to answer that, I said.

I thought of the tall, strong man with the downward smile - whose eyes were so icy they could nearly cut glass. I thought of the man who shot his gun aimlessly when the leaves rustled in the night. I thought of the old man, now, slumped in the cold, blue chair.

My father was the one who taught me how to ride a bike. And then, he would send me off to make money - for him. He was the man who let me drink beer when I was eight - and then, together, we would wait for the fish to bite, swatting away the mosquitoes, but not needing to be anywhere else. He was the man who would leave me cowering in the shadows when he grabbed the old belt from behind the closet door. I was frightened of him. I was obsessed with him.

He had me raking stones on days so hot the sweat would drip like pungent water. If you spoke about God he would slap you - because if you couldn't see it, it didn't exist. In the mornings breakfast would be fresh. In the evenings we ate moldy scraps. And I was never surprised to find him face down on the rotting floor.

There was no routine. I did whatever he thought I should do. Sometimes it was to dig a ditch. Sometimes it was to pull the weeds. Once in a while, when his eyes were clear, he would talk about the math. And his fascination for numbers would make him come alive. He would scribble on napkins and on molding – and on skin. And he would become animated - and his high would soar to levels beyond our existence.

He was a broken man. He was an ignorant man. He would talk to himself, when he thought I couldn't hear - with pictures of her crumpled in his hand. He would wash in the pond - because that was the way we were meant to wash. And he gave no thought to the grime beneath his nails. He never knew luxury. He never wanted to. His life was here, in this deterioration - where she had been, where I had grown.

On the day I finally left, I was still just a boy. And with a single, worn duffel bag tossed behind my shoulder, I tried to hide my eagerness from him. I had visions of grandeur. I had visions of you, long before you came. I would go to New York City. I would change my life, there.

He stopped me at the foot of the door - his hand on my shoulder, his scotch, on the table. *Don't come back*, he said, with a voice so clear, I thought maybe he was sober. And the words, like glassy shards, tore, deep, into my chest. And I searched his face for anything that told me he didn't mean it - for signs that he would miss me; for signs that he was sorry.

But I saw nothing.

I won't, I said. And my voice was cold – but it didn't match his stare.

And I walked away with a heavy heart. But with each step I took, the world became lighter. When I looked behind me one last time, I expected him to have disappeared. But he was still standing there. He was still watching me.

I knew, then, that I would come back. And I knew when I did, the door would be open - and he would be sitting in his favorite green chair. And I knew he would make me breakfast. And that his bottle of scotch would always be the only object free of dust.

In his hesitation to go back inside - to his chair, where his drink was waiting - he told me that he wanted me to come back. For him. But he wanted me to stay away. For me. It was the closest thing to love he had ever shown me.

You were scratching your head. You were waving at the air as if something you couldn't see was attacking you.

I breathed in, deeply. *Why do I love my father?* I repeated your question so that the words could roll off my tongue and become real.

You put on your big, black sunglasses - so I couldn't see your eyes. And instantly, my reflection taunted me.

I thought of the dirty boy, in the middle of Times

Square. I thought of the many days he awoke surrounded by garbage - and coins that people left at his feet. I thought of the jobs, worked hard at - however little they paid. Because he was used to working hard for nothing. I thought of the dark alleys that never scared him - because there were far worse shadows to be caught in. I thought of the dollars that began to add up, and the buried box he kept them in. I thought of the men, walking past him, in their fine Italian suits; and the way that he took notes - and the way he finally saved enough money to buy one. He had a pair of shiny shoes, before he had a bed to sleep in. And he was good with numbers. Excellent with numbers. Soon, they noticed. Soon, they wanted him. Soon, he was taking tests and being stamped with their approval. He had unbeatable drive. He was a ferocious worker. He was charming people during the day and sleeping amongst the roaches at night.

I watched as you gnawed on your perfectly manicured nail. Even you had the ability to be flawed here, amidst the imperfect. We would go home, eventually. And you would sulk for a day or two because your dreams of the old money I had come from had been crushed. And you would look at me just a little differently from now on. But you would stay. Because I had my own fortune. And I would leave you when another, better you came along. But for now, I was under the same spell that hypnotized me when I was with him. And I would indulge in that. I would embrace it.

I don't love my father, I said. And it was empowering to see things so vividly.

You breathed a sigh of relief. You smiled and kissed my cheek. You had decided that it was okay to love me again – that it was okay for me to love you.

But I didn't love you. I didn't love anyone. I couldn't. Because he couldn't. And I only just figured that out.

As we headed back to the house, my gold watch

hidden beneath my sleeve, I noticed the dirt on my shiny, leather shoes; shoes that weren't meant to be worn here. I would wipe them clean tomorrow. Or maybe I would leave them. It didn't make a difference. Because no matter where I was or what I wore, I would always be barefoot in the pea green pond, with him.

I would always be the filthy boy searching for that soaring high, because he made me want it so desperately. I would always be here, pushing through the branches with you just a footstep ahead of me. And I would always be small, no matter how big I got, for I would never stop being my father's son.

5 SITTING WITH GOLD

I was barefoot on the old gray carpeting searching, once again, for the apartment labeled 6B. The black, strappy heels in my hand had done their duty for the night - and after hours of drinking and dancing my feet were aching and my head had surrendered to bouts of dizzying waves. I wouldn't say I was drunk because I was very conscious of everything around me: the cracks in the drywall, the flickering lights, the smell of wet dog - but I couldn't deny that my judgment had faltered - for what was I doing here, now?

The building was an old one, and the upkeep was poor - but that doesn't mean it was cheap, for if you stretched your head out any west-facing window you could see the entire city skyline, and there was a nice park only a block away. It wasn't for the faint of heart, though. It wasn't for a girl like me. It took a certain kind of person to live here. Someone creative. Someone who had the ability to visualize past the broken elevators and appreciate the charm: the brick walls, the old, out of tune piano in the dusty foyer, the literally starving artists who gathered on the front sidewalk to sell their paintings and sketches, because they knew if no one else noticed them, the other, more successful artists residing here would. There was a hot dog stand on the corner which, strangely, became a one-stop breakfast nook early in the mornings - with newspapers, eggs, and simmering sausage. Before the rest of the world awoke, one could leave the building - just as the sun was slicing into the darkness - and be seduced into alertness with the strong aroma of freshly brewed coffee.

When I finally came upon the door, it seemed to loom in front of me - as if I were seeing its reflection in a carnival mirror, disproportional and wobbly. I tapped my hand against it and waited. There was a low buzzing noise coming from the light bulb above me. The sound was ominous - like an eerie film soundtrack - and it prickled at the goose bumps on my skin. I shuddered, searching the long corridor for any signs of life. It wasn't unthinkable to imagine other tenants coming in at this hour - in fact, it was their artistic duty. But, the longer I stood by myself, the louder the buzzing seemed to get, and so I pounded on the door, firmly, pressing my head against the wood.

"Bobby?" I called. Nothing. I reached for the door handle and turned it. It was unlocked. I pushed myself into the darkness, closing the door behind me. I urgently felt my way into the living room and turned on the side lamp. The room glowed, displaying for me the familiar multi-colored polyester couch, the black and white photographs lying on the floor, waiting to be hung - the guitar, gathering dust in the corner.

"Bobby?"

The bedroom door was slightly ajar and so I peeked my head in, squinting past the blackness to see. As my eyes adjusted, I noticed a lumpy shape on the mattress. My chest began to knock. I slid my hand around the wall beside me in search of a light switch. When I found one and flicked it on, the room filled with pinkish warmth. Bobby was curled into a ball, a black cotton sheet twisted around his body - a pillow, between his legs. He appeared to be naked - the multitude of fading arm-tattoos disturbingly more apparent in his fetal-like position. There was a cigarette, still lit, and balancing on the edge of a coffee mug, and a couple of empty vodka bottles lying on the floor. *Tonight's poison.* I walked over to the bed, dropping my shoes into a pile of dirty laundry. I lifted the cigarette, flicked it, and took a quick, ash-filled drag. Then, I crushed it into the wooden nightstand. When the embers had dimmed, I tossed it into the cup with the other blackened butts.

I sat on the edge of the bed and placed my hand on Bobby's chest. I was pleased to feel the slow rising motion of it. *Oh Bobby*, I thought, pushing the damp, yellow hair out of his forehead. *When will I stop this?*

I inspected the small room. There were papers scattered around the floor - one was crumpled under my foot. I picked it up and attempted to iron out the creases with my hand. I recognized Bobby's abrupt handwriting. There was a sentence: *He can be found in the shadows of town, painting his canvas or dancing around.* It looked like lyrics - perhaps the opening to a song. I was sure the other pages would be similar - all marked with hurried words, never ending. I sighed, beginning the task of tidying. I gathered up the papers, one by one, and neatly piled them together. For a moment I held them tight to my chest wishing that Bobby could crawl out of his skin and become more like me. For then, wouldn't things be easier? I placed them on top of his dresser knowing they would only end up right back on the floor. A photograph, leaning against the mirror, caught my eye. It was of us. I picked it up and held it to the light. Bobby had his hair in a ponytail, and he was smiling brightly at the camera - his dimples, prominent, his blue eyes bright. My body was turned away but I was looking straight into the lens - my dark eyes were wide, as if I had been surprised, and my mouth was rounded, as if I were in mid-sentence. My hair had not yet been put through the tedious task of straightening, and so my tight, strawberry curls were abundantly piled on my head like a wild, dirty mop. I snickered. I didn't remember the moment. But, why should I? There had been many random, candid pictures taken throughout the years. Somebody was always capturing something when Bobby was around.

I slipped the photo into my purse. For some reason, I wanted to keep it. I walked back into the living room and sat down. My eyes were suddenly heavy. I would stay for the night. In the morning, I would go to him. *No, in the morning, you will realize that coming was a mistake and you will leave - probably before he even awakes.*

A noise startled me into consciousness. *What was that?* I sat forward, my ears being pulled toward a faint, howling sound coming from the corridor. I stood up and walked to the door. The howling - whimpering, really - was more apparent, now. I peeked out. Instantly, it was silent again. The lights were still flickering but I didn't see anything else. Then, a shadow brushed across the wall. Someone was there. I stepped out, into the hallway, and came face to face with a skinny, pale woman. Her hair was short and black and she wore a white tank top - and men's boxer brief shorts. Her eyes were red and puffy and her nose was running. She wiped it with her forearm.

"Who are you?" she asked.

I thought it was presumptuous. Shouldn't I be asking her that? For all she knew I was sleeping and she had woken me up. I glanced at the lacy, black dress I still wore. "I'm - well, no one."

She laughed through her tears - it was a mocked cackle. "You're no one?"

I didn't like her. I don't know why. If she had been another person - someone in my neat, clean apartment building with the doorman always safely guarding - perhaps I would have asked her if she was okay. But there was nothing about her that was appealing. I wished I hadn't opened the door. "I'm - Dari. Dari Quinn." Why did I give her my last name?

Her eyes cascaded down my body, settling on my legs. "Well, Dari Quinn, aren't you a fancy one?"

I felt the burning in my cheeks.

"You here to save him? Cuz you wouldn't be the first."

Who did she think she was? "Thank you. I know all about Bobby's ways."

"You say it like it's a movie title - *Bobby's ways*. Is he passed out in there?"

I didn't reply.

"He is, isn't he?"

"Look - I don't know who you are, nor do I care. What I'm doing here is none of your business. I'm going back in."

"Wait!" she said, her eyes changing instantly from narrowed slits to wide, glistening pools. "Do you have a cigarette?"

"I don't."

"Bobby does. Please get me one?" Her voice was suddenly gentle - melodic.

I sighed. This girl was a master at manipulation. "Fine."

I ran back into the bedroom, quickly, searching the floor for Bobby's cigarettes. Then, I saw the red and white pack sticking out from under his pillow. I grabbed it and raced back out - just in case the strange girl had any thoughts of entering the apartment.

"Here," I said, holding the open pack up to her.

She slid out a cigarette then lit it with a small lighter she retrieved from her bra. She inhaled, long and slow, blowing out a smooth, thin stream of smoke into my face.

"Do you mind? What's your problem?"

She leaned against the wall. "Sorry." But she didn't seem to mean it.

"Alright. Well - goodnight."

"Wait!" she said. "Can't you talk to me for a minute?"

No! I'm tired and I want to go to sleep. "I'm - I have

to be up early," I said.

"Oh please," she said, clasping her hands together and frowning like a little girl. "Just while I smoke this - please?"

It was the last thing I wanted to do. "Just for a minute."

She smiled. When she did, I noticed that she was more attractive than I originally perceived. Her cheeks were like perky apples and she had a small space between her two front teeth. I suppose a smile has a way of changing a face.

"I'm Genji," she said.

"That's an interesting name."

She shrugged. "Yeah - it's Chinese."

I examined her face. "Are you Asian?"

"My mother was Chinese. My father is German."

I nodded. "Interesting mix."

She slid her body down the wall until she was sitting on the floor. "Yeah - well, who isn't mixed these days? Everyone's mixed. The word *mixed* shouldn't even be used unless you're talking about food."

Was she going to analyze everything I say?

"Anyway - you going to sit down here with me? You're making me nervous - standing. You're so high."

I wanted to remind her that she had chosen to sit down. But, I positioned myself across from her, keeping my legs tightly closed and to the side.

"You look like a peacock riding side-saddle. I can still see your panties."

A peacock? I cleared my throat. "Well - I can see yours, too. Except they're not panties - they're men's underwear."

"So?"

I looked away. The light above had stopped buzzing. "So, why were you crying?" If I was going to sit out here I might as well ask the question.

"I was sad."

"Are you going to be difficult for the entire minute I'm here?"

She took a drag, coughing out the word. "Probably."

"What did you want to talk about?" I asked. Then, I thought of a question. "How do you know Bobby?"

"Whoa," she put her hand up, "What is this, an interrogation?"

I rolled my eyes.

"Bobby's my neighbor," and she motioned down the corridor, though I wasn't sure which door was hers. "Obviously."

"Okay. Well - I was just wondering as you seem to know a lot about the women that come here."

"I mean - I'm not blind. I can see what goes on right under my nose."

"I don't know if this is right under your nose. You aren't in his bedroom. You don't live out in this hallway. Or do you?" *Zinger!*

"Oh come on. I don't need to be in his bedroom to know how he lives. He's an attractive, failed musician. The girls come and go."

I pressed my lips together. I hated the word failed. "Have you ever been in Bobby's bedroom?" If she was going to be direct, so was I.

She laughed. I winced. She sounded like a witch. "Don't be jealous. No. You're more my type than he is."

I felt my eyes widen. "Oh?"

"Does that make you uncomfortable?" she asked.

I raised an eyebrow. "Why should it? What - do you think I live under a rock? You think I haven't met a gay person before?"

"I don't think you've met anyone who isn't straight and narrow like yourself."

"You don't know me. I'm not so straight and narrow."

She nodded towards Bobby's door. "I can see that."

"Are you going to tell me why you were crying or

not? Because I have to get some sleep."

"I was crying because I was sad."

I wanted to wrap my fingers around her throat. "Seriously, you're starting to annoy me."

"I don't know why," she said, her tone matching mine, "That's why I was crying - I was sad. There are many reasons, not one. It's hard to pinpoint exactly which life event I was crying about in the seconds before you opened the door."

"You don't make any sense."

She put the cigarette butt out on the dirty gray rug, leaving a distinct black mark that would probably stay there forever. "Of course it doesn't - not to you, because you don't understand depression."

"So, you're struggling with depression?"

"I mean - it's not a clinical diagnosis."

I took a slow, deep breath. "Okay, Genji, tell me something about your life - something that *may* be the reason for your sadness, now."

"Well, I'm not sad right *now* - because I'm sitting here with you. You're distracting me from my sadness. But if I have to pick something out of a hat, let's go with - my daughter."

"Huh?"

"I said *my daughter.*"

"Your daughter?"

"Are you hard of hearing?"

"It's just - I wouldn't have imagined you having a daughter? I thought - aren't you gay?"

She ran her fingers through her wild hair, then she pulled at it. "My God! Gay people *can* have children! When are you going to come out from that rock you're not under?"

I didn't say anything.

"Anyway - I got pregnant when I was a teenager. In case you don't fully understand - *I had sex with a guy, a member of the opposite sex* – when I was young. And I got pregnant."

"Okay."

"Anyway, she - my daughter - was a plump, red thing - and her fingers were long. And she had tiny, little fingernails - you almost needed a microscope to see them. I named her Mary - because it was a nice, normal name. And I wanted her to have a nice, normal life. Then, I handed her over to a nice, normal couple. And I never saw her again. I think they may have renamed her. But, I guess it doesn't matter."

"I'm sorry," I said. "I suppose you didn't have the resources to keep her?"

"The resources? Hmm - let's see. My father was a tyrant who would slap me if dinner wasn't ready by the time he came home from work. My mother was dead. The guy - the one-night stand - was some jerk I met at a bowling alley. He was older and charming - and he had a girlfriend. He took my virginity, then wanted nothing to do with me. I didn't have my own money - I was only sixteen - so, I would say that's pretty perceptive. I didn't have the resources, no."

"I'm sorry. Have you ever considered therapy?"

"Have you?"

I didn't say anything.

"At this point, I would normally say something really flippant - because the question is so cliché. But - I won't. Because, yes, I've gone to therapy. A few times. But the only kind of therapy that actually does something for me is musical therapy. With me as the therapist."

"Ahh. Like Bobby - you're a musician?"

"Well - no, not like Bobby. Bobby works in a stuffy office all day. Then he comes home and pretends to be a musician. I'm an *actual* musician. I don't have a day job. I sing - on weekends, at a night club in the city. During the week, I'm a cocktail waitress."

"Isn't that kind of like a day job?"

"No, it's not *kind of like a day job*. It's in the evenings, first of all. And - I do it, because I want to get a gig there. I'm biding my time. I'm learning the ropes. It's a bit of a fancier place. So - I'm getting in good with the people. It doesn't count as a day job if you're doing it for your art."

"How can you afford to live here?"

"My dad. As long as I'm not living with him, he's happy and willing to pay. But he's always been real generous with his money. That's about it, though."

"How old are you, Genji?"

"Thirty-one, Dari. Yes, I'm old and living off of my dad. But he needs to be good for something. How old are you?"

"Thirty-three."

"Really? You look younger. Maybe it's because you have a permanent deer-in-headlight look to you. Anyway - aren't you a little too old to be drunk-crashing at Bobby's?"

"I'm not - I wasn't drunk. And yes, I'm too old for a lot of things."

"Oooh - am I going to hear Dari Quinn's sad stories now?"

"You know - you're a jerk."

"Hit me where it hurts."

"Just because I don't moan in the corridors seeking out attention, doesn't mean I don't have my own sad stories."

"Give me one."

"I don't have to prove anything to you."

"But you will - won't you?"

I scratched my lower leg ferociously. I noticed a few bug bites by my ankle. The place was probably flea infested. "What do you want to know?"

"Oh, I see. You're going to throw it back on me. Okay. Tell me about your parents."

I thought of my mother's voice, reading to me beneath the soft lamp. I thought of the smooth, cotton blanket, wrapped around us like a cocoon - and the way she smelled like baby powder. "My mother was a stay-at-

home mom. She was generous and kind. She loved to
cook - and she found a way to use whatever was in the
cabinets to turn our dinners into tiny feasts. And she
loved her children. My father was a laborer. He never
came home with clean hands. And he spoiled us with
love, because we didn't have much of anything else. I only
had one second-hand doll growing up - one - and I shared
it with my sister. But it never felt like I was missing out on
anything because our lives were filled with so much. And
we didn't have a television. Well, we did have one, once -
a used one, but it broke down pretty quickly. Anyway - for
entertainment we would tell stories - after dinner. We
would all take turns. It could be about anything - it could
be a story about the day's events - or it could be
completely made-up. It was fun. There was a lot of
laughing."

Genji grumbled. "Is it just me or does this sound
like a happy story? The theme was sad - remember?"

"You know - you asked me to tell you about my
parents, and I'm telling you. I have wonderful memories
of them - of childhood. I'm not going to deny it."

"Good for you. I feel bad for you."

"Listen, Genji - just because I had a nice childhood,
doesn't mean I don't know pain." I dug my nails into my
skin. "When I was young, there was a fire."

She didn't say anything, but I could feel her inching
forward.

"My mother had been cooking - I'm not even sure
exactly what happened - all I know is that my sister had
called to her. She wanted something - a band aid,
something silly - because my mother liked to baby us - and
my sister, Evie, she just ate it all up. Anyway - my mother
left the pot on the stove - to go to her. She had only been
gone for a moment - something splattered, she had left an
oven mitt too close - something like that. Anyway, the
next thing I know, the kitchen is in flames - and the house
is filling up with smoke. My father and brother were in the

basement - I think they were fiddling around with an old table my father had found on a curb, somewhere - they were trying to fix it up - my dad was good at that kinda stuff - and my brother just loved to assist him." I stopped for a moment. The scene was still so vivid in my mind. I could still smell the burning. I could still feel the stinging in my eyes.

"Go on," she said - as if I was her entertainment.

"I screamed," I said, shrugging, because my eyes were welling up. "I was the first one to scream. I screamed, *Fire! There's a fire!* Maybe it wasn't quick enough. I don't know. But my father came running up the stairs, holding my brother in his arms - and at first, he tried to put it out - the fire. He tried to stop it. But, it was getting out of control and I think he knew it. He was calling to my mom - everything was happening so quickly. He told me to take my brother and get outside. But I wanted to know why he wasn't coming with us. *Where are you going?* I kept asking. And he was yelling at me. *Take him outside - go outside now!* Finally, he ran upstairs - I think the flames even followed him. He was trying to get to my mother - he was trying to get to my sister. I grabbed my brother's hand - he was only seven at the time - and together, we ran toward the street and huddled under a tree. I didn't do anything. I didn't run next door for help. Somebody called the fire department, anyway - because before I knew it people were all around us. I didn't pay much mind to what was happening, though, because I was so busy watching my home fall apart - like a tower of blocks. I was so busy watching the sky light up." I felt weak, suddenly.

"They died?"

I nodded, choking on my words. "Yes, they died. All three of them. Gone. Just like that. I was sitting on the couch, reading. My mother was cooking dinner. My father and brother were fussing with tools. It was an ordinary evening. And we were planning on having more ordinary evenings. Nobody imagined that the next day wouldn't come. Nobody imagined that my brother and I would be separated - each living with a different family." I wiped my face with my hands. I felt my shoulders relax and slump.

We stayed silent for a few seconds. Then, Genji spoke. "Sounds bad," she said, "Sorry." And in her eyes, there was finally sincerity. I understood. She could relate to me now.

"I've gotta get some sleep," I whispered, standing up.

This time, she didn't try to stop me. Instead, she stood up also, ready to retreat, herself.

"They say my name means gold," she said, just as my hand touched the door knob.

"Oh?"

She nodded. "Yeah. Think it's a sign? Like, maybe my mom imagined I would be something big one day? Like, maybe I was meant to struggle now because eventually all my hard work will pay off - in gold. What do you think?"

I shrugged. "I think all hard work pays off. Maybe not in gold, though."

"It helps sometimes, doesn't it?" she asked. "To talk?"

I nodded. "I think I'll to cry myself to sleep now."

"Don't let Bobby catch you. You'll scare him away."

When the door was shut behind me and I was back on the polyester couch, I thought about my strange encounter. I felt like an intruder in my own skin.

"How long have you been here?" It was Bobby, and he was standing at the doorway of his bedroom, a towel wrapped around his waist. His eyes were bloodshot.

"You look exhausted," I said, "Go back to bed."

He walked over to me and sat down beside me. "I see you've been cleaning again."

I shrugged. "What can I say? I like to clean up messes."

He smiled, his face instantly warming me. "You've got to stop doing that."

I sighed. I curled my body into his and he wrapped his arm around me. He smelled like chemicals, and nicotine. "I try to stay away," I said, "But I can't."

He sighed. "Remember what dad used to always say? There's no shame in needing someone."

"I remember."

"So you didn't answer me - how long have you been here?"

"Just a little while. I was on a date. It was fun - to dance and be out. But, the guy was a bit of a bore. And, I was worried about you. You haven't returned my calls all week."

"And you being *you* were thinking the worst, weren't you?"

"Always."

"Do you think your husband would approve of this behavior - going out on dates and all?" he asked.

"I think I'm going to leave him."

He squeezed me. "I think that's a good idea."

We were silent for a few moments. Comfortably.

"I think I just realized that I'm jealous. Of you," I said.

"Come on."

"You're gifted. You're free."

He planted a small kiss on the top of my head. Then he pushed, with his foot, a bottle - perhaps of whiskey. "This," he said, "Isn't free."

I sat up. I felt a headache beginning. "Pour me a drink?"

He nodded, standing. He stumbled back. For a moment I thought he was going to fall. But he balanced himself and began his search for a clean, empty glass. "I can never find anything," he said, "This place is such a dump."

I let my body fall back into the couch, into the warm

spot he had been sitting in. "This place," I said, "is not so bad."

6 CARRYING THE HAPPY FROG

I was driving my shiny, silver Toyota when I pulled up behind an old blue pick-up truck. At first, I didn't think much about it. I was playing with the radio stations. I was fumbling through my pocketbook, looking for cough drops. I was feeling a bit under the weather. I was tired and sore - and the red light was lingering just a little too long.

I felt the moisture filling up my bra. I felt the hair sticking to my face. Damn air conditioner. Damn you! Of all days to take a drive like this. Of all days - with a broken air conditioner and a two hour ride ahead of me. I was annoyed. I was bored. So, when my mind started wandering, I found solace in the eyes of a stuffed, green frog happily sitting in the back window of the vehicle in front of me. For a moment, I was brought back to my childhood - to the lavender room, the frilly bed skirt - the piles of stuffed animals that collected dust in the closet, and the corners, and atop my twin sized bed. This made me smile. And because I smiled - despite the traffic and stifling weather - I felt compelled to know more about the driver; the owner of the frog.

I couldn't see his whole face but in the side mirror I

saw his wide jaw-line and the shadow of a thickening, tawny brush. I saw overgrown hair. Maybe brown - or lighter. His hand was lazily tapping the outer door - perhaps to the beat of a song. It was a thick hand - a worked hand. His forearm pulsated with every movement and he wore a ring on his middle finger - a silver ring - or perhaps white gold - and it shone against the sun, its reflection scattering.

I drove for a while behind him. Not because I was following him. But because we were simply going the same way. I watched his hand go in and out of the car window – sometimes with a cigarette. Every now and then he would glance into the rear view mirror and I would struggle to guess the color of his eyes. They were small eyes - squinty eyes. And I imagined them to be blue. That was my guess. He was a man, older than me, with dark blue eyes. He was in the business of manual labor - perhaps a plumber or a carpenter. I noticed the mud - or, rather, stains of mud on his large, thick tires. I decided he was a farmer. Somewhere in North Jersey. The tires, with their permanent stains, had been driven through muddy terrains regularly. He was a blue-eyed farmer from Jersey.

When he turned onto the highway, I decided it was fate. We were going in the same direction. There was a reason I had pulled up behind him. There was a reason I felt compelled to stay close to him - not letting others come between us. I just didn't know what that reason was. Temporary insanity?

He wasn't driving very fast. The other cars were flying past us, but we maintained our speed well. He wasn't in a hurry. He had patience. How refreshing! Myself, I had no tolerance for slow drivers. Normally, I'd be hitting the horn and cursing aloud for no one to hear. But there was something about driving, lazily, behind him with the mountains and the forest whisking by us. It was hypnotic.

Finally, he pulled into a rest stop. I convinced myself

that I, also, needed a rest and I followed him into the small parking area. There were gas pumps and vending machines and bathrooms. *What am I doing?*

He parked his truck close to the road. I parked two spots away from him. When he got out, he stretched. He wasn't tall, but he wasn't short. Perhaps just under six feet. And his hair was just past his chin - unkempt and dirty-looking. He leaned against his truck and lit a cigarette. Then, he spit into the road. If I had been back home, in my everyday frame of mind, I would have been disgusted. I would have possibly even admonished him - sometimes, I was outspoken like that. But there was something about the man. I imagined him with a wide-brimmed hat and a strong horse. He was a man's man. Yet, I saw something else. I saw him lifting me over a puddle. I saw his hands, calloused and rough, stripping away my panties.

For a minute, I lingered near my car pretending to be preoccupied with my nails. Then, I began walking closer to him. I wanted to see his eyes. When I was just a foot or two away, he spoke without looking.

"You following me, ma'am?" His voice was low and deep - almost monotone.

My heart quickened. "Excuse me?"

His eyes pierced into mine. They weren't blue. They were green. One eye was darker than the other. But they were green just the same. He had fine lines spreading out from them - and a small scar just by his temple. But, his cheeks were smooth and his skin was a deep biscuit color. He wore a simple t-shirt, worn blue jeans and thick-soled boots. He was a man in great shape, but not because he cared about his image - he didn't appear to care, at all, about the superficial things. He was a man, fit, because he worked hard.

"You following me?" he repeated.

I looked down at my feet. My toenails were pink and my sandals were white, like my blouse. My jean-shorts seemed *too* short and I suddenly wondered if I had the figure to carry them. "I'm not sure what you mean?"

He put his cigarette to his mouth, there was a glimmer in his eye. Was he mocking me? "You've been behind me since that light back there - before the highway. I turned in to get you off my tail."

A giggle erupted from my lips. "I'm sorry to disappoint you. But, I think it's just a coincidence."

He took two more drags from his cigarette - quick ones, as if his life depended on it. "It's no coincidence." But his tone stayed the same. There was no sign of anger or annoyance. Just curiosity.

I thought about running quickly back to my car. But, that would be silly; strange. *Any stranger than this?* "I had to use the bathroom," I said.

He tossed his cigarette-butt onto the asphalt, then crossed his arms in front of him. He had a way of watching that rendered me immobile as much as I wanted to disappear. "Try again," he said.

Like a force pulling me in, like a school girl, afraid to be punished, I found myself drawn to his directness - to the boldness of his accusation. "I mean, I *did* notice you," I said, surprising myself, "in front of me. But, really, I was going the same way."

He took a few steps toward me. I could smell the tobacco. I could see myself running my fingers across the prickly bristles around his mouth. "Where you from?" he asked.

"Me? Oh - Long Island."

"What are you doin' out here?"

"I was helping a friend of mine. She just moved. She doesn't know anyone. I was helping her unpack - getting her settled."

"Do you have a name?" he asked, still examining my face.

"Sarah."

He began to turn away from me but his eyes continued to linger. "I'm going to use the facilities," he said, "If you're still here when I get back, I'm takin' you for a ride." He waited for me to reply, but I said nothing. "You might wanna walk them pretty feet of yours right back to your vehicle - before I make you dishonest."

I felt the warmth filling up my body like an instantaneous lighting of a thousand tiny matches. I watched him walk away slowly, carelessly, a box of cigarettes sticking out of his back pocket. A welcome breeze drifted through then, cooling my damp skin. I felt inert. The thoughts were scattered in my head. *What am I doing? This is silly, dangerous - waiting here for him.*

It seemed like hours had passed before he reappeared. When he was close again, I saw that he was smiling. It wasn't a broad smile, like the one I couldn't seem to hide. It was a soft smile - a teasing, lopsided smile, which fit him, which seemed to animate his face perfectly, as if he had never fully smiled in his life and didn't need to.

"Let's go then," he said, as if it weren't a big deal - as if I were simply an old friend. I found myself pulling my body up, into the passenger side of his truck. It was dusty. There were ashes scattered about and empty water bottles littering the floor. A couple of tools – a wrench, a hammer and a screwdriver – were lying on the back seat. I closed the door firmly. And as we passed my shiny, abandoned car, I couldn't help but despise it.

When we were back on the road again, I spoke. "Where are we going?" I asked.

He adjusted the rearview mirror. He put an unlit cigarette to his lips and left it there without lighting it. "You'll see."

I didn't feel nervous. I didn't feel scared. I felt something I hadn't felt in a long time. Excitement. Perhaps this feeling was similar to the high one can experience from bungee jumping - or race car driving. Extreme sports. I never understood them - I always thought, *How silly! Why risk your life?* But, now, here I was with this stranger - and he could be anyone, he could do anything - yet, I was immersed in the rush of the unknown - in the thrill of our unexpected, little game.

After a few minutes we pulled off the main road and onto a small trail. It was a bumpy ride and the trees hovered around us. Branches were hitting the windshield; pebbles were flying into the air. It was a desolate area, and the fear began creeping into me, slowly. I glanced into the side mirror - it had a crack in it. The busy road could no longer be seen.

We pulled up to a small, brown house nestled in the center of the woods. It had a covered screen porch that ran the entire width of the house. And there was no walkway, only weeds and sticks and leaves.

"Is this your house?" I asked.

He finally lit his cigarette and jumped out of the truck. He walked over to my side and pulled open the door for me. Then, he reached his hand out and waited for me to take it. I leaned into his body and he lifted me out. I smelled the soapy dirt.

"I stay here sometimes," he mumbled.

I followed him through the screened door. When we entered, I inspected our surroundings. There was a small faded couch on one side of the porch. On the other, there was clutter - boxes, books, a table-saw and a pair of dirty brown boots.

"Don't mind the mess," he said, continuing through, into the living area.

This part of the house was a little neater. It was a simple set up with a gray love seat and two chairs that matched only each other. They seemed to be made out of a thick, coarse material - and they were multi-colored, with wild, bright hues. On the other side of the room was a stove, a refrigerator and a small table with two chairs.

"Beer?" he asked.

I wanted a vodka and seltzer with a slice of lime. But I had a feeling I wouldn't be getting that here. "Sure," I said.

He opened the fridge. From what I could see, there was beer, a small bottle of milk and not much of anything else. He pulled out two cold bottles and opened them, easily, with his hands. He set mine down on the table. I reached for it. I took a small, quick sip. The cold, bitter liquid tasted better than I imagined it would. "Thank you."

He nodded, settling down into one of the chairs. I followed his lead, taking the chair directly across from him. I wasn't sure what to say.

"What's your name?" I asked.

He scratched his chin. "It doesn't matter. We both know why we're here. You want something. And I wanna give it to you." And for some reason, nothing he said came out condescending or vulgar. It was simply said because it was true.

"Why?" I asked, "I mean - why do you want to give it to me?" I wondered if we had the same *it* in mind.

"Because you didn't leave when you had the chance."

It wasn't the answer I wanted. "Not because - there's an attraction?"

He sat back in his chair. "I don't know you."

"I don't know you, either." Was I fishing for a compliment?

"You're a pretty girl," he said. "Different."

"Different?" I asked.

"From the others - around here. And elsewhere."

"Oh," I said. "Well thank you." It was nice to hear, I suppose, considering I always felt quite average, with my mousy-brown hair and small, unimpressively pale face. Then I thought, *Maybe he means different in a weird way.* "I think you're different, too," I said, "You know, from the men I'm used to being around."

"Well, they're probably wearin' their panties too tight, then."

I laughed. "I think maybe you're right."

There was something about him - something in the

eyes, in the laughter held back, that told me he was kind - a good person. But perhaps he had been hurt; damaged. I found myself wanting to let him rest his head on my lap. The different emotions were bubbling inside of me. I wanted him to throw me up against the wall. And then, I wanted to sit behind him in a hot, bubbling bath and wash his hair - and soap his back.

"Are you going to tell me anything at all - about yourself?" I asked.

"Like what?"

"Well - you don't want to tell me your name. So, I'm afraid to ask."

"Jut ask – and you'll find out," he said.

"Okay. Are you married?"

He shook his head. "Think I'd be here with you if I was married?"

I shrugged. "Maybe." Then, I decided I liked the mystery. I would stick to simple questions. "You like music?"

He nodded. "Sure. I like music. Music's good. Music helps."

"Helps?"

"With everything. With life."

I nodded. "It does."

"You hungry?" he asked.

I was - a little, but I couldn't possibly eat. And I didn't think he had food to give me anyway. Perhaps he was just asking to be polite. Although, he didn't strike me as someone who engaged in petty prattle. "No. Thank you."

He nodded, his eyes lowering to my neckline and lazily resting there. I felt my breath quicken – and a sizzling in my belly. It was as though he were touching me - as though his thick fingers were slowly tracing the curves of my skin. I took another sip of my beer - a gulp, actually, a long, heavy gulp.

"Whoa," he said, "Slow down. There's no rush."

Actually, I did have to be home. I had chores to do. I had errands to run. I still had a long ride ahead of me. But I didn't say any of that. Because I wanted to be here. I wanted my life to come to a halt.

"Can I see your bedroom?" I asked. And I heard the hoarseness in my voice.

He searched my face - his eyes moving quickly, studiously. He stood up. "It's back here."

I followed him to the back of the house where a small room with large windows waited for us. He had a double bed with a simple white sheet strewn over it. I walked to the foot of it, running my fingers against the cloth. I felt him watching me from the doorway.

"I'm being quite forward," I whispered, "I know."

He didn't say anything. But, after a moment, I heard him entering the room and slowly walking toward me. When his breath was on my neck he lingered there, perhaps enjoying the scent of my torture. I didn't doubt that he saw, clearly, the trembling of my skin - the yearning inside of me. And so, when I felt his soft lips upon my neck - the scratchiness of his beard against my skin, I let out a sigh - a sweet air of relief. His hands rested on my waist as he planted small, idled kisses behind my ear and on my shoulder. I felt my body leaning into his and his hands began their exploration. With great care, his fingers trailed their way up to my hair and he piled my curls upon my head. He held them there as his tongue danced along the nape of my neck and I heard the whimper escape me, and it made his hands move slower - to my shoulders, to my belly - to the curve of my breasts. Then, suddenly, with one swift movement, my blouse was off of me, and he was pulling down my bra. I turned to face him. His eyes, blazing, told me that he, too, was drowning in his want for me; that it was taking all of his willpower to hold back. I pulled his shirt up, over his head and tossed it onto the floor. His chest was firm, the pale hair scattered; the scars, jagged and long, not taking away from the beauty of him. I unzipped my shorts and wriggled out of them. He groaned, pressing his body into mine. I fell back, onto the bed. He stood over me, his hands resting on my thighs. "I need this," I whispered. And, oh – how I meant it! His lopsided smile returned. He twisted his fingers around the string of my panties, pulling them, quickly, until they tore. Then, his skin was against mine - his chest pressing into my nipples, his mouth pressing into me. His hair swept along my skin as his urgent lips moved quickly from my mouth to my neck, from my belly to my thighs. He was biting and tasting; savoring and taking. When finally, he shook his pants off in hurried, breathy desperation, I was digging my nails into his skin. I was begging him for more.

Later, as the sun was setting, we sat on the covered porch – he, wearing only his shorts, me, wrapped in a thin, flannel blanket. The beers, warm now, were resting in our hands and the sound of the trees rustling against the late day breeze made heavy, my eyelids.

"You've got a long ride ahead of you," he said, his golden hair disheveled and damp.

I nodded. "You kicking me out?"

"No," he mumbled, "No - you're welcome to stay the night if you'd like."

It was a nice offer. An offer I could see myself taking. I envisioned myself safe and snug and curled within his arms - against the warm nook he'd create for me, my softness tainted against his hard and damaged skin. I stared at the thin wedding band on my finger. I twisted it. "I can't," I said. "But I want to."

He nodded. "You mean you won't." But, again, his words weren't bitter or harsh. They were simply factual.

I held my breath. "I'm married." I winced, certain he would disapprove.

He took a long sip of his beer. Then, he stared out past the bushes, somewhere deep within the forest. "I know," he said.

I suppose it was foolish to think he hadn't seen my

wedding band. He clearly wasn't a man who missed much. But he *did* seem like a man who would care - who had morals. Unlike me. The adulterer.

"Are you mad?" I asked.

"No," he said, simply. "Just wonderin' why you're here. So far from home. With me."

I shrugged, realizing how crazy it all seemed. "My God, I don't know," I put my hand to my mouth, grinning behind it. "I really don't know. I guess you were right - before. About wanting something. I guess I needed this." I shook my head, admonishing myself. "I don't even know your name."

"Your man, back at home - will he be wondering where you are?"

I thought of the cell phone lying on the passenger seat of my car. I don't even think I locked the doors. "He will be. Shortly," I said.

He nodded. "I'll take you back, then." He went to get up.

"Wait," I said, motioning for him to sit back down. "Not yet. I just want a little more time."

He nodded. He sat back.

I realized that his actions were just as crazy as mine. He didn't know me, either. I was just some stranger on the road - some person, following him on the highway. He saw, in me, something I had only just realized in myself - in my unwillingness to leave. I was just as lonely as he was, but I wasn't alone, like him. He knew I was married, immediately. Of course - didn't he say he'd make me dishonest? He gave me an opportunity to choose. He gave me a minute to think. Perhaps he needed to be needed. Perhaps I was his good deed for the day. For, wasn't it a good deed - to fill someone with life?

"Tell me about your scars," I said. And I stood. And I went to him, positioning myself on his lap. He welcomed this intimacy, easily. He pulled me close, wrapping his arms around me, deeming the flannel unnecessary, but ensuring I was covered, all the same.

"You don't need to know about them," he said.

"I do," I said, "I want to know."

He kissed the side of my mouth, softly. "You smell so fresh," he said, "So clean."

I closed my eyes, allowing the limpness of my body in his hold. "Tell me," I said.

"It will unclean you," he said. "I don't want to do that."

It was the sweetest thing I ever heard - the softest words, I'm sure, ever to be formed from hardened lips, like his.

They say that love can happen in an instant. And I never really believed in that. But, perhaps, here, on this canvas chair, with the fresh air and billowing leaves; perhaps here, it was possible to fall in love with someone whose name was a mystery; whose story would stay untold.

"Your eyes," I said, touching his brow with my finger, "They're aged." The sea of green was mixed with swirls of faded brown, and they were weary and sparkling, all at the same time.

"It's what happens," he said. "Life happens. Not to you, though. Not the hard life."

"Where's your family?" I asked. "Do you have family?"

He surprised me with an answer. "I have a son. He lives with his mother, somewhere in the mid-west."

A son. The thought of it pinched at my heart. "I guess you don't see him."

"Not since he was two years old. His birthday just passed. Last Wednesday. He turned ten. I bought him a toy frog. Don't know why. He's a bit old for that. It was just sitting there - in the store window. I never sent it, though. Wouldn't know where to send it, anyway."

I thought of the happy frog sitting in the back window of his truck. It would travel with him everywhere. He kept it because he needed something to hold on to.

I wondered about the mother. He wasn't married now but had he ever been? Had she been a stranger - someone he met on the road, like me? Or was she an old love - a first love; the kind that remains, always? I didn't ask, because he wouldn't have told me.

"You don't think you'll ever try to find him?"

He shook his head. His face shadowed.

The darkness was beginning to fill the corners of the room. The light was starting to disappear. We both knew it was time to go.

I held his face in my hands. I studied his eyes. They were dimming - the gleam, fading. It was the only moment I truly saw what I had given him; what I would be taking away when I left. I brushed my lips against his, slowly first - then quicker and deeper as his hands reached into my hair bringing my face into his. Afterwards, when all was still, our lips didn't part. Instead, we stayed connected - the sweetness of our breath mixing; the dampness of our faces saturating each other.

I didn't say anything else as we drove back into the woods and headed for the highway. Instead, I watched as the little brown house got smaller and further away, eventually disappearing amidst the tall trees and thick shrubs - and darkness. It was as if it never existed. It was as if it had appeared only for us - and now it was useless; hibernating. I felt a pull in my chest.

When we finally got back onto the highway and the cars were speeding past us, he put his hand on my knee and squeezed it. Then, he spoke. "Don't get caught up in this," he said, "In today."

I sighed. "It will be difficult to forget."

He lit a cigarette and rolled down the window. "Wanna drag?" he asked.

I surprised myself by taking one. The thick, sharp smoke choked me and I coughed, violently, for a few, long seconds.

"Why'd you take it then?" he asked.

I shrugged. "I don't know."

He shook his head. "I can see what you're doin'. There's a line," he said, "that shouldn't be crossed. You don't need to cross it to get to the other side. To get what you want. Know what I mean?" He waved at the car behind him – the one at his tail, to pass. "Anyway, if you can't find it on one side, you're not gonna find it on the other." I watched his face, shimmering against the street lights. I closed my eyes, memorizing him. I was afraid to look anymore. If I did, I wasn't sure I'd get out of the car. "I've done it," he said, "My whole life. I can't even see the line anymore. I crossed it a long time ago. Now, there's no goin' back."

I understood.

The sound of the horn made me jump and I winced as the sun shot into my eyes, waking me from my fantasy. I threw down my visor and my vision was clear again. The traffic light had turned green. The truck in front of me was far ahead and the car behind me was urging me to go. I stepped on the gas, speeding to catch up until I was directly behind the blue truck again. I felt titillated. I felt ridiculously sad. I stared at his fingers, still tapping on the door. I stared at the smiling, stuffed frog in the window.

When the exit for the highway came I held my breath. I turned my blinker on. But the truck proceeded past the exit, continuing on straight. As I turned, gradually, I watched as the man and the frog got further away from me - like the little brown house in my mind. *Bye*, I whispered.

When I was on the main road, my cell phone began to ring and it tore into my thoughts. I hit the button on my dashboard. My husband's voice came through the speakers. "Hey - you on your way back?" he asked.

I smiled. "Yes, yes - I just left a little while ago. I'll probably be home around dinner time - maybe a little before."

"Okay," he said.

I heard the commotion in the background - the children were yelling, or maybe they were laughing. It was that bittersweet sound - the noise that never left, the noise that had become a part of us. "Do me a favor?"

"Sure - what?" he asked.

"Can you call that babysitter - the one that came the evening we had my work dinner? Her number's on the fridge. I think."

"For what? When?" he asked. And his voice was hurried - as mine always was. I understood. The kids were pulling at him. Or fighting with each other. Or spilling something. Or simply needing his attention.

"For tonight."

"Oh?" he said, relaxing. "Where are we going?"

I looked at the wedding band on my finger. I never took it off. Yet, I never paid much attention to it either. It had simply become one with my skin. "We're staying in," I said.

7 THE PALE GIRL

Daniel had been watching Peggy Winters through his telescope, which had the ability to focus directly into her living room area - for she rarely closed her curtains, which were sheer, nonetheless - and her windows were tall and wide, nearly the entire width of the space. He saw her only in a tiny world; one where nothing else, but her, existed. And she, at twenty five, was tall and slender with barely any curves, no hips at all, and a straight, flat chest, and a perfectly arched back - and hair, so pale, it appeared, to him, white; and she wore it, sometimes, in long, tight braids. To him, she was an illusion - a delicate, fluttering ghost. And in her, he was transported - to a time of cranberry pie and yellow, floral tapestries - and mama's homemade gravy.

He had first come upon her by accident. He had returned home from the food mart, tired and moody - for the walk had aggravated the pain in his leg and it was shooting up to his hip. He had thrown his bag of oranges onto the copper, tray-table - a treasure he had picked up on a trip to the Middle East with June, years before her death. *The Bedouin have used this kind of thing for centuries*, he had said to her, *Look, you can lift the tray off and on, easily*. But she hadn't been impressed. Nothing much impressed her. In Puerta del Sol, in front of the great bear statue, she had wrinkled her nose. *It's just a bear and a tree*, she had grumbled, shrugging it off. The Grand Canyon, in all its splendorous layers of red rock, was *dangerous*, in her mind - *silly*, was another inappropriate word she had used. He often wondered why she married him at all. Even in youth, they had nothing in common. Her life had been a series of moaned complaints. She had complained until an hour before she died - and then she was silent only because a seizure had rendered her mute.

It was these very thoughts that ran through his mind as he settled into his favorite yellow chair, mumbling to himself - and to June, her deeply lined, chipmunk face, admonishing him, even in spirit. He removed his new white sneakers - wondering why he allowed the salesman to convince him they were necessary - and pulled off his sweaty socks, the smell, instantly foul. It was there that he noticed the purple blackness on the sole of his left foot. His blood sugar had been high again - he knew this. He had been careless with his health, already having lost a toe. And as much as the loss of his toe had left him feeling dejected - causing him to sit in blackness, night after night for a month - he hadn't changed his habits much. And so, the sight of the gangrene didn't surprise him, only exasperated the emptiness that had been eating at him for nearly a year.

The telescope had been a gift to himself, after he had lost the will and ability to travel the way he used to. It was his retreat. And, before the diabetes had taken control of him, he found great comfort in stargazing. He was limited, here, with the tall buildings and intrusive city lights - but, he had a place in the country, only a short hour's drive, where the night would explode into unending brilliance and he could lose himself in the watch - in Jupiter's stripes, in finding the Orion Nebula, high within the southern sky. There was some comfort to be taken from the idea that there was, in fact, something bigger. It allowed him to have faith - to believe in the possibility of an afterlife. And so, he much preferred using the telescope in the country, where the universe had the ability to give back. But, it wasn't practical anymore. He needed to be closer to town - where the supermarkets and the medical facilities were just within reach. So, he had taken up people-watching. There was a park down the road, across the way, where - if he moved his telescope well enough to the right - he could get a clear vision of a good part of it. And there families would picnic by the trees, and dogs might be running, and children played.

On this day, though, the first day he saw Peggy, it was cloudy - it was dark and grey; a day in which moods were sunken and people felt less guilty about staying indoors. He had pleaded with himself, from the confines of his body - the foulness of his necrosis still permeating the air - to fight against the pressing shadows. He had mustered up the willpower to stand; to hobble over to the window where the scope stood, beckoning. It was then, as he scanned past the swinging tree branches, the dark, red brick and motionless, drawn shades, that he came across a bright, open window - and a woman; Peggy Winters. Although then, he didn't yet know her name.

She was a vision of purity. She, in a white leotard and leggings, her snowy hair cascading past her shoulders, was attending to tasks - simple tasks around the living room. And every movement was graceful - as if she had somehow mastered the ability to become one with the air around her, with the objects: the lifting of a cup, the reaching for a book; the random positioning of her body into a plié - as if she weren't going to allow life to get in the way of her art; of ballet.

Daniel's breath caught in his chest. He felt suddenly ballooned, instantly sedated. And his fascination puzzled him, for he had seen the Cliffs of Moher, and he had seen Dubai from the top of Burj Khalifa. He had been lucky that way. His childless existence had allowed him the freedom to travel - to see the magnificent wonders of the world. People, though, had always fallen short for him. Like June, they had always been intrusive. So, here, a woman was sipping on water – and plucking grapes with only her mouth. And he was frozen. And he didn't know why.

The girl became a part of his life. In the mornings, his eyes would open just as the sunlight was spilling into the room. Suddenly, there was something to look forward to. Suddenly, waking was the way it had been in youth - bursting with promise and the idea that there was still much more to be discovered. He would stand in front of the full-length mirror and be astounded by the reflection of an old man - a bloated, short man, with only wisps of white hair barely covering his freckled head. The skin on his throat was sagged, so much so, that he could grab a handful of it, easily, and shake it as if he were cupping a quivering mass of jelly. This man was nothing like the man he was inside. That man, the younger him, never appeared to lack in anything, for he was well traveled, and he, before the recession, had been generous. People didn't easily notice his flaws - for instance, his stubbornness, or his quick temper - because they were forced to focus on that, which overshadowed the ugly. He had always been able to ensure it.

And so, in front of the window he sat, day after day, watching the girl and her idiosyncrasies - the fact that she liked to walk around in only a tee shirt, the half-eaten cereal bowls she left on the coffee table, the undergarments, lacy, colorful things, strewn across the dining table. She, unlike June, had no sense of shame; no sense of separation between that, which was personal and should remain hidden, and that, which was appropriate in a common area. It intrigued him, this rebellion - this *way of living*. She was childish, sometimes, immature. And then there were days she morphed into a woman, with sheer, layered fabrics and high heels, and lipstick.

Sometimes, she would walk to the window and stare out into the day. In those moments, he would be able to make out, perfectly, the details of her face: the deep, wide-set eyes - the only darkness she possessed, the porcelain skin, the high cheekbones without even a hint of color, the prominent jawline and nose - just a bit longer than one would imagine. Her face was like a statue, in its plain perfection; it was a face needing to be painted. She was like the Mona Lisa - not so beautiful in the typical sense, in the proportions and subtleties of classic beauty, but she was handsome in her distinct features. She was strength and fragility all mixed together.

One evening she had a male visitor. Daniel felt the rush of heat to his face as he watched the tall, lanky stranger. The boy towered over the girl, yet, he seemed small in comparison - awkward. They went from standing, oddly far apart, to sitting, almost near each other, but not quite close enough. Oh, how he wished he could better see her face! He studied the boy - the dark features, the dungarees and casual shirt, as if he were home watching a football game! *Imbecile! Not good enough!* And on that day, Daniel didn't sit at all. Instead, he stood, clutching the telescope, waiting for the inevitable shame to occur. But there had been no cause for concern that day. And when, finally, the stranger left, Daniel slumped into his chair and slept, not dreaming.

The next day, Daniel took a long, hot shower – much longer than his usual quick cleansing. It was nice to stay under the water, allowing the steam to envelope him; it was something he rarely allowed for. And he imagined the girl, in her casual routine, experienced that sort of self-pampering, regularly. When he was finished, he retrieved a small black comb from the kitchen junk drawer and, after carefully dipping it in water, he combed what little hair he did have, neatly, to the back and side of his head. Then, from his bottom dresser drawer he located an old bottle of aftershave. Being that he didn't have cologne, it would have to suffice. He splashed it, generously, onto his face and neck, patting firmly at the loose skin. It stung a little - for his skin hadn't been privy to chemicals in many years, he rarely even soaped it. But the slight prickling sensation enlivened him and he welcomed it.

He dressed, quickly, choosing brown trousers which were just a bit snug around his belly, and a patterned, collared shirt. Then, he chose a suit jacket from the back of the closet, despite the radio warning of another hot day. He covered his bad foot with baby powder, than wrapped it in an ace bandage. He wanted to put on his old loafers but they just wouldn't fit. So he settled for the white sneakers.

When he stepped outside, he was pleased to find a warm breeze sailing through the air. And he sucked in the day's musky, garbage scents. Funny, how the mind can change ones outlook on things! He stood, for minutes, simply staring past the whisking cars, to the large, golden doors beneath the awning across the street. Somewhere past them and high above the ground, the girl lived. Today would be the day he learned her name. The idea of it - of being able to call to her - jolted something inside him so powerfully, it brought a deep aching to his chest. He would have to be careful. He would have to take care. There comes a time in a man's life when he must refrain from certain excitements, for - as lovely as they are, as freeing and exhilarant - they can prove fatal.

He waited until the street was clear then quickly crossed, ignoring the pain - not in his foot, for there was no pain there, as his nerves had been damaged - but in his leg. When he reached the other side, he was unsure of how to proceed. He hadn't planned well. He walked past the golden doors, peering into the foyer. He saw only his reflection. He lingered for a short while, directly in front of the glass - then, deciding it was too obvious, settled for a spot against the red brick, just past the doors. He glanced across the street - to his window, to the small balcony he never used, the one without a flowerpot or a chair. Someone came out then - a dark-haired woman and a child. He repositioned himself - he moved forward, wondering what to do. But they brushed past him quickly, no care, at all, to his intentions. He began to pace as people hurried by him - park-bound people, people moving in and out of the building. He watched the sun as it did its slow dance across the sky - and, he remained, even after it had become hidden by the structure.

A man, chubby and well dressed, began to pass him. For a moment it appeared he was going to address Daniel. Daniel smiled, hoping the man would say something - start a conversation. But he didn't. Instead, he stopped in front of the entryway, frantically fingering his cellular phone. Daniel frowned. *The world has lost its ability to communicate!* When, finally, the man reached for the handle, the door opened and the girl, in all her breathtaking splendor, appeared. She was lovely in a silky green and white dress, and her hair - her ashen hair - was loosely twisted at her neck, her slender, ostrich neck. She smiled at the man as they passed each other, the man suddenly attentive and aware of her. "Afternoon, Peggy," was all he said. But his eyes didn't leave her. And she smiled, brightly, unshadowing the sidewalk. "Hello," she said.

What a voice! It was more than Daniel had imagined! And *Peggy* - darling, sweet Peggy - that was her name. It was like a song - what was it? Peggy Sue? Oh, how close he suddenly felt to her. He knew her so well - more than others, he was sure. He knew her habits, the things she did when she was alone. And now, he knew her name. Oh, if only she would look at him - see him, then she would know, too, all that he held for her.

But she passed him, easily, not glancing his way at all. He struggled to smell her - to know her scent. But she was down the block so quickly - too quickly - and he found himself reduced to watching the way her dress fluttered in the breeze and the outline of her long legs moving beneath it.

He waited a little while longer - until the door opened again. Then, he entered, quickly, as if he were an occupant. He stood in the foyer, the simple, dark foyer, with the benches and the mailboxes and the elevators in front of him. He made his way to the metal slots - scanning through the names. When finally, he came upon a *Peggy*, he smiled. It was her, he was sure of it. *Peggy Winters*. That was her name.

Now, in present time, it was autumn of the following year and Peggy's male friend had been joining her more regularly. And Daniel had lost two more toes. The deformity had originally made him contemplate suicide - for how disgusted would Peggy be? How revolting was the sight of him?! Even the lanky one - *the boy!* - would be more appealing now! And he thought of taking the entire bottle of his medication at once and mailing a letter to Peggy explaining how he'd miss her and how he was leaving, to her, all of his possessions.

But slowly, little by little, as his life continued to intertwine with hers - as he sat with her, as he twirled with her, as he napped with her, drank with her, ate with her - the thoughts of suicide subsided. And she, once again, became it all.

On one particularly crisp day, when the park's grounds were free of people and they had covered with an abundance of colorful leaves; when Peggy, appearing to be sick, sat in a plush white robe near a pile of crumpled tissues, Daniel, whose day had gloomed with hers, decided he would send her flowers.

He pulled out the big, yellow book and flipped through the pages until he found a nearby florist. He dialed the number and waited. A cheerful voice - a man's voice - came on the line.

"Yes," Daniel said, "I'd like to order a bouquet of

flowers. I want them delivered. Today."

"Certainly - is it for a special occasion?"

"It's for a lady friend. She isn't feeling well."

"I'm sorry. I hope she feels better soon."

"Yes, well - it seems she's gotten a bit of a cold - a runny nose. She's been lying around all day. She's a dancer, you see - and she practices all the time - mostly at home - but, she has no energy today. None at all." And it felt so good to be able to talk about her. It felt natural.

"A dancer. How nice. What kind?"

"Ballet. It's only a hobby. She likes to read a lot, too. She's not the best cook. She orders in quite often. I would say she has pizza at least once a week - one would never imagine, with her figure, the way she eats."

The man cleared his throat. "What can I send her for you?"

"I'd like a large order - as big as you can make it - of white lilies. Do you have them?"

"Beautiful. Yes. I'll make it special. I'll throw in some Queen Anne's lace ...,"

"No. Nothing. None of the lace. None of that child's breath stuff, either. It has to be only white lilies. Alone. Simple. "

"Are you sure? Because really - the curly willow makes it."

"I don't even know what curly willow is. But either way, I don't want it. White lilies. Alone. A lot of them."

"Absolutely. What should I write on the card?"

A card? Daniel thought of it. He smiled, imagining her face when she received his gift. "Well - I suppose you can start with her name - it's Peggy."

"Yes."

What would be enough? "Peggy, I'm sure you'll know why I chose the lily. There isn't another flower in the world that better represents you. I hope by the time you receive this, you'll be feeling much better. You are lifeless, today - and this complete lack of energy saddens me. I hope my gesture brings a smile to your face. When you are well I'd like us to talk. Especially about your gentleman caller. You can do better. We both know it. Don't let him taint you. There are brighter things waiting for you. Good day, my sweet girl."

The voice on the other end was silent for a moment. Then, he spoke. "You don't want to shorten it a little?"

"No - did you write it down? I want it to be word for word."

He heard the man shuffling papers. "I think I have a slightly larger card - I'll fit it in," he finally said. "And, who shall I write as the sender?"

"No need. She'll know." And wasn't it true? In her heart, wouldn't she know?

Later, he waited behind the lens, humming softly so that Peggy may better rest. Her hair was matted and limp and one pale leg was the only part of her to emerge from the robe and it hung, limply, off the side of the couch. He wanted to lift it, gently, and cover it Perhaps he should have sent her soup - or a new book to read. One would think the boy - with all the time he's spent - would be tending to her. *Imbecile!*

When finally, he saw the florist's van double-parking on the street below, Peggy had gotten up from the couch and disappeared into another room. He hoped she wasn't vomiting into the toilet - it was possible that she didn't merely have a cold; that it was something worse, like the flu. He held his breath, waiting for the delivery person to make his way to Peggy's door. Minutes passed. Finally, Peggy reappeared, freshly showered - her hair, damp, the robe gone and replaced with what appeared to be an oversized jumpsuit - perhaps flannel. Daniel frowned. It was out of character for Peggy, to dress in attire fit for a man. It engulfed her! Then he thought of the lanky boy. *His clothes?!* He tried to recall the boy's visits. Each time, after hours of drinking wine and what appeared to be mindless chatter, she had walked him out of the room.

Daniel had assumed she'd gone to the doorway - where they said their goodbyes. But the doorway was not in his view. Nor was her bedroom. Is it possible she had been sharing her bed with him? *Damn girl! Fool!*

He watched Peggy clear away the crumpled tissues. Then, something distracted her - the doorbell, he assumed. She left his sight again. He waited, impatiently, a simmering rage festering inside of him. When she returned, she had the flowers with her. He examined them. The bouquet wasn't as large as he wanted them to be - he would complain about this tomorrow - and they were in a vase, not wrapped, like he expected. He hoped it wasn't plastic - he despised the cheapness of plastic vases. He scanned her face. She was smiling. She was putting the flowers to her face. He closed his eyes. He breathed in, slowly, with her, imagining her scent - the airy, sweet fragrance. He would forgive her.

He watched as she tore open the card. Her face was brighter - he was sure of it! He had done more, with this gesture, than the imbecile had ever done with his cheap wine - or with any of the indiscretions he had committed against her. Daniel had decided that she had been vulnerable - and the boy had taken advantage of that.

Peggy stood by the window brushing her hand across the flower tops. She was reading the card. She was pleased. He could see it! He had succeeded! But then, the crinkling of her face began - a sudden slumping of her shoulders; a frown. What was this? She put the card down and twirled a lock of wet hair around her finger. It was an anxious move - an insecure move; quite unlike her. She began to pace back and forth, hastily. Then, she stopped at the window again. This time, she was searching. For him. He stepped away from the window. What now? He pulled the drapes closed. She wouldn't be able to see much, anyway - not well, at all, without a telescope or at least a pair of binoculars. But, he stayed out of sight just the same.

What was he afraid of?

He would have an early dinner. He would distract himself. He went to the refrigerator and opened it, inspecting the contents. There was some unwrapped cheese, a half carton of eggs and a bottle of sparkling water. *Dammit!* He would have to go food shopping in the morning. He took out the eggs and the cheese. He would make himself an omelet.

He ate slowly, all the while staring at the closed drapes. The apartment seemed dismal, now - eerily empty. He imagined what Peggy might be doing. Perhaps she was back on her couch with the tissues - the surprise, easily behind her. Of course! She wasn't angry. She was simply taken back! Once she relaxed and had a moment to admire the beauty of the flowers - she would understand! She would be grateful! With each thought, his fork moved quicker.

When his pan, dish and glass had been dried and put away, he pulled open the drapes and positioned the telescope. He scanned her living room. It was empty. Where were the flowers? Had she put them in her bedroom? He liked the idea.

He waited. He noticed a new picture on the wall behind the couch. He wondered why he hadn't seen it before. It was hard to make out the details, but it appeared to be framed in silver. He liked the way she arranged it - off center, not aligned, at all, with the picture above it. That sort of thing would have driven June crazy. He snickered at the thought of it. How he wished June could have known Peggy. Perhaps, if she had seen how easily Peggy lived - how simply she went about her days, June would have appreciated the life he had given her more. He knew that, had it been Peggy he married, his memories would have been much different. Peggy would have been in awe of the places that June took for granted. She would have been happy with him.

The sun was disappearing. The street lamps had come

on. One by one, the windows in the building across from him were lighting up. Peggy's apartment was blackening. Perhaps she had run out for medicine, or to get something for dinner. He would wait.

He was as calm as he'd ever been. He had become used to sitting in the dark, listening to the ticking of the wall clock. The pain in his neck felt like the perfect sacrifice. It felt necessary. And he trained himself to endure it; to have patience. He felt strong, despite his debilitation. He felt new.

Finally, Peggy's home lit up and as quickly as the warmth filled his body, it left him - for she wasn't alone. The boy was with her.

Daniel ignored the pool of sweat that was starting to form in his armpits, in his pants. *What betrayal!* It was he, who had brightened her day! It was he, who had sent her the flowers! Yet, the *imbecile* would receive the reward! "Damn you, Peggy! Damn you to hell!" he yelled out.

His breathing was labored. *Shame on you, Daniel! You're no worse than the boy when your temper gets the best of you!*

He watched as Peggy embraced the boy. It was a feeble embrace. *So weak he is! So young!* Where was the fortitude? Where was the gravitas? Then, her hand went to the boy's face and their lips came together. Daniel's nails dug into his skin. His eyes didn't leave them.

When they parted, Peggy walked to the window - away from the boy, toward Daniel. She seemed to be looking directly at him. She seemed to be trying to say something - to tell him, with her eyes, that it wasn't the boy she loved. He felt the anger seeping out of him. "Come, my dear. I'm right here," he whispered. "I'm waiting."

Suddenly, he was cold, trembling, but the perspiration was so heavy it was dripping off of him. The pressure, then, began slowly, like pins needling into his arm. Then, the sharpness started in his shoulder. He stood up quickly. "Shucks," he said. But his own voice sounded foreign to him. The crunching in his chest began - the squeezing, it was unbearable! "Peggy," he whispered, as the lights in the distance faded. And he reached for her; for the drapes, the velvet, burgundy drapes that June had picked out when they bought their first house. When he fell backwards he brought one panel with him. And it covered him, on the floor where he became as still as his surroundings; where the slightest hint of a smile remained frozen on his lips.

On the other side of the street, in an apartment occupied by a woman named Peggy Winters, there was a man putting up blinds across the large, living room window. His fiancée, Peggy, was sipping on a glass of merlot, leaning back into her fluffy, green couch.

When the man was finished, Peggy Winters walked to the window and stared out at the twinkling lights in the distance; at the building across the way.

Then, she closed the blinds.

He can be found
In the shadows of town
Painting his canvas
Or dancing around
To the people that pass
It's the beauty they see
Of a gentleman laughing
So wild and free

And his colors ignite like a powerful force
And he rides like a knight on his ivory horse
But the make-up it covers an old, jagged scar
And he rides towards the sunset but never gets far

8 DISCUSSION

In Dear Roger, Christine struggles with the dissatisfaction in her life. Do you think she has caused this, herself? Do you agree with her decision to leave her husband? What did her affair with Sean signify? How do you feel Roger will react when he reads her letter?

In Losing a Buck, Maxton and Brooke are both writers meeting, one day, at a cafe. How do you view their relationship? Why does Max push Brooke to finish her novel? Do you think he crossed the line when he handed her journal to the publisher? Do you agree with his decision to end their relationship? Do you think it was the right thing, for Brooke, in the end?

The story, An Incredibly Dismal Saturday, is based on the author's own childhood memories. Did you find there was a story being told? If so, what did it say to you? How does the title relate to the story?

Barefoot in the Pea Green Pond is about a successful young man heading back to his childhood home to visit his father. He is accompanied by a woman he is dating. How do you view their relationship? Why is it so important for his date to meet his father? What do you make of his revelation at the end? Do you think it is warranted? How do you envision his future?

The story Sitting with Gold finds two women who randomly meet in a hallway. What kind of affect do you think each woman has on the other? Do you believe Genji was merely seeking out attention before Dari came out? What is your perception of Genji? What do you make of Bobby - and how does each woman view him? What kind of relationship does Dari have with Bobby? In the end, Dari says that Bobby's place "isn't so bad". Why does she say this?

In Carrying a Happy Frog, a woman, Sarah, is driving and notices a stuffed frog in the window of the truck in front of her. Why does the toy ignite a sudden interest in the driver of the truck? At the end of the story we find out that she had imagined her entire interaction with the stranger. What do you make of Sarah and her life? Do you believe fantasies can teach us things we cannot find in the reality of our everyday?

In the Pale Girl, we find a man in the later years of his life. Why does he develop a fixation on Peggy? What kind of life did he live as a younger man? How do you view the relationship he had with his late wife? What are your thoughts about the ending?

ON THE BIG WHITE OAK
INTRO

The woman sat in front of him, steady and precise. She was not yet seventy but she looked every bit her age, if not older, because her skin was deeply lined and her eyes appeared wilted, as if they were missing an important element; as if they had long been unfed. Her hair was white but well managed, perfectly combed, and she was aware of all of this; she knew herself well.

"I suppose you think you're going to fix me," she said, examining him, intimidating him. Her lips were tightly pressed together. She disapproved, it seemed. Perhaps she saw inexperience. Perhaps she was envious of the years he had ahead of him.

"Actually," he said, "I don't fix. I help."

"I see," she said. Then, she yawned. She looked out the window. "How old are you?" she asked. There it was. But then, there was something else - something dark in her eyes. He thought: She's known much pain. Then: I've seen her somewhere before.

He cleared his throat. He had done this, the throat-clearing, six times so far. It was a nervous habit. She made him uneasy.

"Nearly forty," he said. She would be surprised. She would have thought him younger, as did everybody. And then, he thought: She can't imagine me so inexperienced now. But wasn't he?

The woman smiled, confusing him. It was the kind of smile he liked, big and face-changing. It gave her back a bit of her youth. "Forty," she repeated.

He nodded. "So, tell me - what brings you here?"

She didn't answer him immediately. She was trying to figure him out. He shifted in his seat, wondering if she was doing it purposely or if this was how she interacted with everyone, cautioned and scrutinizing.

"This sounds like a job interview," she said, "Are you looking to hire me, perhaps?"

He laughed. It was forced. "I'm just trying to figure a beginning."

She adjusted her clothing, picking lint off of her black pants; brushing imaginary particles off of her simple white sweater. He noticed the nail polish on her toes, peeking through her shiny leather shoes. It was pink and fresh. He thought: Impeccable.

"I wanted to talk," she said, "I just wanted to talk."

For a moment, he was sure he heard a stumbling in her voice; an uncertainty that he didn't think she had. This weakness made him sit up straighter. "What's on your mind?" he asked.

She put a cigarette to her mouth and motioned for a lighter. He retrieved one from his desk. When he approached her, to light it, there was a scent; something familiar. But then, it was gone, and he was back at his seat, watching her.

She inhaled deeply and closed her eyes for a few, long seconds. "I didn't always smoke, you know."

"Oh? Why did you begin?"

"Boredom," she said, "I started about ten years ago. I like it. I should have done it sooner."

He thought it odd. He knew of people, older people, who had resigned themselves to the fact that they weren't going to quit. But, not without regret. He had never come across someone who began smoking later in life. He said none of this, though. It wasn't his job to give an opinion.

"When I was young," she said, "I was in love."

It was progress, he thought. An old love, a lack of closure - this is what she wanted to talk about. "Tell me about it."

She reached into the black, leather bag that sat beside her feet. She fumbled, momentarily, until, finally, she took out what seemed to be a book. It was brown and thick. She placed it on her lap and opened to the first page. He noticed the doodling and the swirled writing. "A journal?" he asked.

She nodded. "There's so much to talk about - my memory fails me. It helps."

Part I

Chapter 1

It was a plastic table that her mother set up, and a big sign that said: *Lemonade*, and Marian sat, by herself, watching the lemon halves float, lazily, against the pale liquid that sparkled beneath the hot July sun. Her hair was brown and uncontrollably curly and the spirals ended just past her shoulders, some strands sticking to the sides of her face as beads of sweat began to form. She was freckled, on her nose and cheeks, and her mother found it cute. But she hated being cute. And she hated freckles. And she wished, many times, that she looked more like her striking cousin, Delia, who was just like a sister to her, but different than her because people paid attention to Delia and not so much to Marian.

The old Victorian house across the street was one of many in the quaint little village of Babylon, Long Island. It was white with wide, red doors and green shutters and it had a large wrap-around porch, which held an old wooden rocking chair that she swore sometimes rocked when the wind was calm and no one but her was watching.

The house had been vacant for some time now and she often wondered when someone would occupy it. She dreamed of a girl living there - a young girl, her age. And the girl would have long blonde hair, a contrast to her own dark features, and she would love lemonade stands and kickball - and the two of them would become inseparable.

She sighed. The empty street showed no promise of customers, only the glaring, hot pavement that would burn her feet if she walked on it barefoot, and the houses with everything closed - the doors and windows, because people had their air conditioners on. She saw two birds hopping, daintily in front of her. One of them seemed angry at the other – lunging at it, its melodic voice becoming seemingly frantic. Moments later they flew away, one right behind the other, and Marian watched as they glided, effortlessly into the bright blue sky. *I bet they're the best of friends,* she thought and smiled at the idea of it, *best friends may argue, but they never stay cross for long.* She closed her eyes, imagining the birds, a whole bunch of them, surrounding her, landing on her shoulders and her head. She heard the whistling, the singing. Then, another sound disrupted her thoughts.

There was a large, white truck coming down the block. Its angry motor was out of place – unwelcome. She frowned, impatient for it to pass, when it started to slow down, then stop, in front of the empty house.

She watched a few men jump out. These men were loud, talking and laughing, too loud - like the truck.

They began to pull things out: boxes and some chairs, and as they did this, their chatter seemed to dissipate, and then they were moving things from the truck to the house. Quickly, against the heat, they were fanning themselves and wiping their foreheads. Then, they became quiet in their discomfort; in their work.

She took a sip of lemonade, and it wasn't cold anymore. She looked at the pre-filled cups in front of her. The ice had melted. The ice was melting in the pitcher, too. She wondered about calling to the men and telling them: Here, drinks for you! And she imagined them smiling at her, patting her back and saying things like how nice it was, for her to think of them, and about how delicious the lemonade was.

But she wouldn't call to them. There were many things she saw in her head that she could never actually do in real life. Even in school she kept to herself and didn't make friends easily. She was sensitive, they told her, and a bit of a tomboy, and the other girls regarded her as strange - like a creature from another planet, because dolls didn't interest her, neither did pretty dresses. Delia was her closest friend, surely by default because she was family, and Marian treasured the weekends she spent sleeping over Delia's house, and she did so at least two weekends every month. And it didn't bother Marian that Delia's bedroom was filled with all kinds of dolls: porcelain dolls that couldn't be touched, squishy dolls for sleeping, dolls that blinked, dolls that talked, dolls that had long, silky hair, which Delia liked to brush. And it didn't bother Delia that Marian never played with the dolls.

Two years ago, when Marian was five, she had a loss - her father. He died in his sleep. A brain aneurism, they had said, and her mother didn't stop crying for a whole month. Since then, it had only been the two of them, but Rosa (Marian always called her that) never seemed satisfied with Marian. She never understood about dirty fingers and soccer balls, and so Marian tried, really tried, to wear the dresses that Rosa constantly bought for her, but she was never in them for more than ten minutes before they were stained and Rosa was cross. Constantly, her mother would compare her to Delia. "Why can't you be more like your cousin?" And Marian would shrug. She didn't know. "Be a lady, Marian! This stuff you do – it's for boys!" And Marian didn't really understand why.

Rosa was born in Lima, Peru and came here when she was eighteen. She met Robert, Marian's father, only a year after she arrived - and they had both insisted the love was instant.

Robert had been of Irish and German descent, with pale skin and dark eyes, and he was a Certified Public Accountant, who performed audits for the Internal Revenue Service. He took his work seriously, something Rosa admired, and he was distinguished - a cultured, educated being. Six months after they met, Rosa became pregnant with Marian and feared she might lose him. But he had already purchased the simple diamond ring he was going to present her with and when she told him the news, he was ecstatic.

After his death, Rosa was scared that she might be looked down upon – an uneducated, foreign woman with a child and no husband. In Peru, Rosa never made it past the eighth grade and it was one of the many insecurities she hid. But she was a fiery woman who people respected. She was intelligent and blunt, but also a bit sheltered; a bit naive in her views. Only her sister, Delia's mother, who had married an Italian business owner, truly understood the struggle and the determination to blend easily into the North American culture.

Now, Marian turned to see her mother's round face, staring at her through the window. Her thick, black hair was piled loosely on her head, and she smiled at Marian, and waved. Marian wished she would go do something else and waved back, quickly, then turned her attention back to the men.

They seemed to be taking a break. They stood, casually, around. One of them stretched his arms above his head, as if he were only just waking up. Then, a shiny, black car pulled up in front of the house causing them to disperse. Marian felt a stirring in her belly.

A man got out of the car, first, and he was very tall, and he was smiling. Then, a tiny woman emerged, and she had blonde hair, cut to her neck, and she had a cool energy that Marian could feel from across the street. The woman pointed at something and she was speaking loudly and very quick, like a teacher Marian had known once; a teacher she hadn't liked at all. The woman appeared to be displeased about something and she was shaking her head, walking swiftly past the men and into the house. The tall man, on the other hand, stood back, talking with one of the movers, his hands in his pockets, his face calm - and for a moment, he tilted his head back in laughter. Then, another figure came out of the car – a smaller figure. Marian stretched her neck to see. She was sure that it was a girl about her age, she noticed the long, yellow hair blowing in the breeze. She wondered: Has my wish come true?

The girl was bouncing a ball - perhaps a tennis ball. And she seemed competent with the object; focused. Marian watched as the ball smacked into the sidewalk and then flew back up, as if suctioned into the girl's grasp. Then, the ball hit the ground too hard and went flying over the car, toward Marian.

Immediately, Marian ran to get it, because now she had a reason to say hello. But the girl was quick, too, and standing in front of Marian just as Marian realized the ball was in fact a tennis ball. When she looked up to give it back, to meet her new friend, she realized that the beautiful long, yellow hair was not attached to a girl at all - but a boy.

His hair was down to his shoulders, she had never seen a boy's hair so long, and his skin was gold-like, maybe from the sun, and he had big, blue eyes, twinkling eyes. She felt herself blushing. She wanted to turn away. But he spoke: "How much?"

She didn't understand. "What?"

"For the lemonade. I'm thirsty."

Marian had forgotten all about it. "Fifty cents," she said, and she pointed to the sign. "See - fifty cents."

He crinkled his forehead and his lips tilted into an almost-smile, a look he would carry with him way into adulthood. "How old are you?" he asked.

"I'm seven. I'm going to be eight next week. July eleventh."

"Figures," he said, shaking his head and taking the ball from her. "Well, I'm nine and a half. If you were older, you'd know that people are getting at least a dollar for lemonade these days."

Marian was surprised. "A dollar? For one cup?"

He began bouncing the ball again. "Sure. Just in the summertime, though."

"Well - of course. Nobody sells lemonade in the wintertime."

"That's cuz there's not a need for it. People aren't thirsty as much in the winter as they are in the summer. In the summertime people are hot from the sun, they get dehydrated and that makes them thirsty. When there's a need for something you can raise the price." Then his eyes widened. "I betcha you can get a dollar twenty five!"

Marian shook her head. "Nobody will pay that much."

"I'll prove it," he said.

Then, the tall man came up from behind him. "Time to go, Adam," he said. Then, to Marian, "And what's your name?"

"Marian Brown," she said, feeling shy. She looked at her feet.

Adam interrupted. "Can I have some lemonade, Dad?"

His father nodded, reaching into his pocket. He took out a dollar. "How much, sweetie?"

Adam answered for her. "It's a dollar twenty-five, Dad."

Marian's felt her heart beating fast, but she didn't deny it. She only hoped the man wouldn't notice the big sign behind her. She kept her eyes at her feet.

The man, though, took out another dollar. "I don't have any change," he said, then winked at her. "Keep the rest as a tip. And Marian - it's nice to see a kid out here, trying to make some money." She nodded. He started to walk away. "Five more minutes, son."

When the tall man was back across the street, Marian giggled. "Wow," she said, "I can't believe it!" And she handed the boy, Adam, a cup of lemonade. He drank, quickly, then crumpled the cup in his hand.

"I told you," he said, smiling brightly.

"You're really smart," Marian said.

Adam shrugged. "I have to go now."

"Wait." Marian held out the dollar. "This is for you. It's only fair, since you helped me."

He took it. "Thanks," he said. Then, he raced away.

Marian watched until he disappeared into the house. When it was only her and the moving-men again, she heard Rosa's voice from behind her.

"Why don't you come inside now, sweetie?"

But Marian shook her head. "I'm just going to stay out here for a little longer, okay?" And a feeling she couldn't explain, began fluttering within the pit of her belly.

ABOUT THE AUTHOR

Corrine is the author of the novel: On the Big White Oak, and the novelette: Grey Blue. She has been writing since she was a young girl, finding inspiration in the people around her and the complexities of relationships, which have always interested her. She maintains a vast collection of poetry, stories and songs, claiming to write something every single day. She appreciates the idea of delving, deeply, into the human mind and prefers to focus on emotionally challenging subjects, stating that perfectly happy endings 'just don't interest her'.

Corrine is a stepmother and a wife, residing in New York with her husband and their pets. She considers herself a homebody with great family values who loves good food and being surrounded by many voices.